**"All right,"** he said t
**toward the door, "th**
**good-night and turn**

Connor was almost at the threshold when he heard her call after him.

"Connor?"

He turned around quickly, thinking that she had remembered something she needed. "Yes?"

Gratitude was shining in her eyes as she said, "Thank you."

The two words caused sunshine to filter all through him. He hadn't felt like that since they were kids in high school.

"My pleasure," he told her.

The next moment he pulled the door closed behind him and then he was gone.

"Well, we did it, Jamie," she whispered softly to the child, who was asleep in the nearby cradle. "We escaped. Now all we have to do is figure out what to do with the rest of our lives."

Dear Reader,

After writing over two hundred and eighty stories, I'd like to get a little personal.

On Easter morning, Audrey, the very best dog in the whole world, passed away. We got her from the German Shepherd Rescue Society when she was eighteen months old, and we had her for ten years and three months. Despite being badly abused, Audrey had a wonderful disposition.

The second day we had her, I got a call from my son. He needed a tray of lasagna for a Christmas party at his fraternity. Since I never just made one tray, I made one for him and one for our dinner. Leaving the tray on the stove to cool, I drove to USC and then hurried home to feed Audrey. I raced into the family room and put her dog food into her dish. Only then did I see that she'd pulled the lasagna tray off the stove and devoured it while spreading the contents all over the kitchen and family room. She also "recycled" the lasagna by pooping all over. I looked at her in horror and thought, "What have I done?" because I was the one who'd pushed to get another dog. But we soon had her trained, and to her credit, she never took any other food that wasn't given to her. She was obedient and loving to the end.

Audrey is going to be a hard act to follow.

Thank you for letting me share this very personal story, and from the bottom of my heart, I wish you someone to love who loves you back.

*Marie Ferrarella*

# A BABY FOR CHRISTMAS

MARIE FERRARELLA

HARLEQUIN® WESTERN ROMANCE

Recycling programs
for this product may
not exist in your area.

ISBN-13: 978-0-373-75785-5

A Baby for Christmas

Copyright © 2017 by Marie Rydzynski-Ferrarella

Printed in U.S.A.

*USA TODAY* bestselling and RITA® Award—winning author **Marie Ferrarella** has written more than two hundred and seventy-five books for Harlequin, some under the name Marie Nicole. Her romances are beloved by fans worldwide. Visit her website, marieferrarella.com.

**Books by Marie Ferrarella**

**Harlequin Western Romance**

*Forever, Texas*

*The Sheriff's Christmas Surprise*
*Ramona and the Renegade*
*The Doctor's Forever Family*
*Lassoing the Deputy*
*A Baby on the Ranch*
*A Forever Christmas*
*His Forever Valentine*
*A Small Town Thanksgiving*
*The Cowboy's Christmas Surprise*
*Her Forever Cowboy*
*Cowboy for Hire*
*The Cowboy and the Lady*
*Her Mistletoe Cowboy*
*The Cowboy and the Baby*
*The Rancher and the Baby*
*Twins on the Doorstep*

Visit the Author Profile page at Harlequin.com for more titles.

To
Audrey,
The Best Pet
In The Whole World.

Ten Years Wasn't Nearly Long Enough.
We All Miss You
More Than Words Can Say.

## Chapter One

It was so quiet, he could literally hear himself breathe.

Maybe he needed to get a dog.

Connor McCullough frowned and shook his head.

That was the thinking of a desperate man, the twenty-eight-year-old rancher told himself. He shouldn't be desperate. After all, he had earned all this peace and quiet. Lord knew he'd worked hard enough for it over the years.

The only trouble with peace and quiet was that it was, well, *too* quiet. And *peaceful* could also be another word for *boring*.

For the last twenty-eight years, the ranch house he was sitting in had seen more than its share of bustling activity—as well as its share of sorrow. His mother had died here giving birth to Cassidy twenty-three years ago and this was where his father had passed away, as well. The latter had happened a week before he was about to go off to college. The first one in his family to actually *go* to college.

That dream wound up being temporarily shelved, or so he told himself, because if he *had* gone off to college,

Cody, Cole and Cassidy would have been farmed out to foster homes, most likely separate ones.

So he'd stayed on and the four of them had worked as hard as they could to eke out a living and keep the ranch, his father's legacy, going.

It definitely hadn't been easy.

At times it was damn near impossible, but somehow, they'd always wound up managing, thanks to hard work and the kindness of their fellow neighbors in Forever— especially Miss Joan, the redheaded, wisecracking, dour-faced guardian angel who ran the diner that had been, and still was, the small town's only restaurant.

Looking back, he kind of missed those years. Missed working so hard that he fell into bed, bone tired and asleep before his head had a chance to hit his pillow.

Missed hearing his siblings arguing about whose turn it was to do what chore.

At times, he recalled, it had gotten so noisy, he couldn't hear himself think.

Well, he certainly could hear himself think now. But all he could really think of was that he missed the arguing. Missed all the sounds of a family living together.

One by one, Cody, then Cassidy and finally Cole had found the one they were supposed to be with and they had all gotten married in what seemed to him to be, now that he looked back, an amazingly short amount of time. All three were now married with kids. And, of course, they were all here every Sunday. Sunday dinners were pure bedlam and he loved it. But in contrast it made the rest of the week feel almost as quiet as a tomb.

At least, that was the way the evenings felt.

Most of the time Rita, his housekeeper, was around. The woman wasn't exactly a chatterbox, but she *did* talk on occasion and the sound of her voice took away the oppressive feeling of loneliness.

But Rita had gone to visit her sister in Austin for a few days. He didn't miss her cooking—although the woman did have a spectacular knack for making *everything* she put her hand to taste good. What he missed, now that the others were gone, was her company.

Granted that Cole was here during the week, helping him around the ranch, but when six o'clock came, Cole was gone.

Which was as it should be. He wanted his siblings to have families of their own. Wanted them to be happy.

For the last few days, with Rita gone, if he wanted company when the sun went down, he turned on the television set. But somehow, that felt way too artificial to him.

He needed to communicate with something living and breathing. Which was why he'd started entertaining the idea of getting a dog.

Finishing up dinner—Rita had prepared several casseroles for him before she'd left—he began forming a plan. He'd go into town tomorrow and get a cup of coffee—maybe even lunch—at Miss Joan's and ask her if anyone's dog had had pups recently. If anyone would know, it would be Miss Joan. The woman was the unofficial source of information for the whole town. He could swear that she had a way of knowing about things before they even happened.

He liked that idea, Connor thought as he took his lone plate from the kitchen table to the sink.

Turning on the hot water and dabbing some liquid hand soap onto the dish, he smiled to himself.

A dog.

Okay, so most of the time he had more than enough to do around the ranch, even with Cole's added help. But once the sun went down, he could stand to have a pair of soulful brown eyes looking up at him for—

Connor turned off the running water and listened, his dirty-blond hair falling into his eyes. He pushed it back.

Was that knocking he heard?

He gave it to the count of five.

Nothing.

Shrugging, he went back to rinsing off the solitary dish, as well as the knife and fork he'd used. It was the middle of the week, no reason to believe that—

He stopped and turned off the water again, cocking his head toward the front door, the direction of what he perceived was the source of the sound.

This time, rather than just standing and listening to see if he could hear it again, he wiped his hands on the back of his jeans and went to the living room.

No point in wondering whether or not there was anyone knocking on his door when he could just as easily open it and check if there was anyone there.

"You're a little more than one year away from turning thirty. That's too young to be hearing things and imagining people on your doorstep," Connor upbraided himself.

He was definitely going to talk to Miss Joan about getting a dog.

Although he didn't hear any further knocking, Connor still twisted the doorknob and pulled open the door just to make sure there was no one there so he could put his mind at rest.

He wound up doing the exact opposite.

## Chapter Two

There weren't very many things that could catch Connor McCullough off his guard these days. One of the reasons for that was a great deal had happened in the last year and a half.

Cody had shown up with a newborn whom he'd helped a stranded mother-to-be give birth to in her dilapidated, stalled secondhand car. Not all that long after that, Cassidy had turned up, dripping wet and clutching a baby she'd helped rescue from the river during an unexpected flash flood.

And then Cole had topped both of them when he'd brought home twins who had been left in a basket on the doorstep. He had almost tripped over them when he'd walked out of the bunkhouse one morning.

All in all, Connor would have been the first to say that he didn't think there was anything that would surprise him anymore.

With that in his mind, he was in no way prepared for what he saw when he swung open his front door to look outside.

A wan, breathless Amy Donavan was standing on

his doorstep, holding what looked to be a six-month-old baby in her arms.

For a moment, he thought that he'd somehow managed to fall asleep in the kitchen and was dreaming this, or hallucinating it, or whatever it was called when a man's mind conjured up an image of the only woman he had ever loved standing on his doorstep, looking utterly helpless and needy.

"Amy?" he asked uncertainly, half expecting the sound of his own voice to wake him up.

Except that it didn't.

And then his hallucination spoke.

"I'm sorry, Connor. I just didn't know where else to turn." Her eyes, those beautiful, mesmerizing blue orbs that he always used to get lost in, were now the eyes of a woman who looked as if she was on a first-name basis with fear. "I'd understand if you don't want to let me in," the petite strawberry blonde added hesitantly, already taking a step back from the doorway.

"Maybe you might, but I wouldn't." Connor took hold of her elbow and drew her into his house.

Once she was in, Connor closed the door behind her and then did something that he normally didn't do because he lived in Forever, where everyone trusted everyone else. He locked his front door.

Connor turned to look at the young woman, still stunned that she was actually here.

It had been a little over five years since he had seen her. A little over five years since Amy had left town. At the time, she'd been swept right off her feet and hopelessly in love with Clay Patton. Handsome to a fault, self-assured to the point, many felt, of being cocky, Clay was the town's "bad boy." He had a tongue that was dipped in honey and could sweet-talk the feathers off a pair of lovebirds.

When it became clear that Amy was falling for Clay, Connor began to worry about her. Worry about her getting hurt. But Amy seemed to be so genuinely in love and so determined to make things work between Clay and herself, he just couldn't find it in his heart to stand in her way.

So he didn't.

He also didn't tell her how he felt about her.

Instead, he played his part as a steadfast friend, wished her well and told her that if she ever needed him, for *any* reason at all, all she had to do was pick up a phone and call him. No matter where he was, he'd find her and be there for her.

All this time and she hadn't called. Instead, she'd come in person.

The Amy Donavan who had left town floating on a cloud and full of dreams was a far cry from the wan, frightened-looking young woman he saw standing in his living room tonight.

Ushering her and her baby over to the sofa, Connor coaxed, "Why don't you sit down, Amy?"

Very gently, he had her take a seat on the sofa. It was almost like handling someone who was sleepwalking. "Can I get you anything?" he asked. "Some tea? Something to eat? Maybe some milk for the baby?"

The word *baby* seemed to snap her out of the temporary daze that had slipped over her the moment she sat down on the sofa.

"My baby," she said as if she suddenly realized that she was holding the child in her arms. She pressed the tiny bundle to her chest.

Lord, but Amy appeared incredibly weary, he thought. He was afraid that any moment, Amy's arms might give way and she'd wind up dropping the baby. "If you'd like to put her—"

"Him," Amy was quick to correct. "My baby's a 'him.'"

"Him," Connor amended without missing a beat. "If you'd like to put him down, I've got a cradle in the back bedroom down here. You could put the baby in there and give your arms a rest," he told her tactfully.

Connor's eyes washed over her. In his estimation, Amy seemed beyond exhausted. Not only that, but she looked like she'd lost at least ten, maybe even fifteen, pounds since he'd last seen her. Life with Clay Patton had not been good to her.

She gazed up at him, instantly alert because of the suggestion he'd just made.

"A cradle," she repeated, coming to the only conclusion she could. "You have a baby."

Why else would anyone have a cradle? She was stupid to have thought that life had been put on hold for everyone else after she'd left Forever, she admonished herself.

"Oh, I'm sorry. I didn't mean to intrude," Amy apologized. Holding the baby against her, she was already struggling to her feet. "I just—"

The baby began to whimper.

"No, I don't have a baby," Connor assured her as he lightly took hold of her arm and then gently urged her to sit back down on the sofa.

All the fight had been taken out of her long before she'd walked into Connor's living room. Consequently, when Connor tugged on her arm, she practically collapsed onto the sofa. But she continued tightly holding on to her child.

"I have a cradle," Connor told her again, then set her mind at ease. "But I don't have a baby."

The reason for the cradle was a story for another time. Right now, the immediate problem was getting Amy to tell him what she was doing here after such a long absence. And why she looked so beaten down and frightened.

"I'll bring the cradle out," he offered. "You can set the baby down in it and have that cup of tea I promised you. It'll do you good. And once you've finished your tea, you can tell me what this is all about."

"Connor, you don't have to…" Amy began, not wanting to make him feel obligated to go out of his way for her.

Rather than stay and argue with her, Connor disappeared into the side bedroom and fetched the cradle he'd mentioned to her. Carrying it out, he placed it on the floor right next to where Amy was sitting.

And then he stood in front of her, his eyes indicating her son.

"May I?" he asked.

Not waiting for an answer, he very gently took the whimpering baby from Amy's arms. Rather than place him into the crib, Connor held the boy for a moment, gently rocking him and whispering something in the baby's ear that Amy appeared not to make out even though she had moved to the edge of her seat.

As if by magic, the baby stopped whimpering and fussing. The next second, he was cooing and making happy noises. The boy settled down as Connor placed him into the cradle.

"It's got runners," he pointed out to Amy. "So you can rock your son while I get you some tea."

She did as he told her, all the while staring at the baby in the cradle. Much to her relief, he looked contented. She was amazed at how calm he had become.

"What did you say to him?" she asked. "He hasn't been this calm in weeks."

"I just seem to have a knack with babies," Connor called out from the kitchen. Within a couple of minutes, he walked back in carrying a mug of tea for her. "I guess after all the babies that have been through here, it's a talent I just developed."

"All the babies coming through here?" Amy repeated, clearly puzzled. She had no idea what he was talking about.

He realized there was no way she could know what had been going on here recently.

"Long story," Connor told her, handing Amy the mug and sitting down beside her.

"I like long stories," Amy said, taking the mug with both hands. The warmth that seeped through as she held it felt oddly comforting.

"And I'll tell it to you," the six-foot-tall rancher promised gamely. "Right after you tell me yours."

She took a long sip of the tea, letting the soothing, hot liquid fortify her. It never occurred to her to put him off. Connor had been her best friend once—and she really needed a friend now.

"Oh, Connor, I don't know where to start."

"The beginning is always the best place," he said kindly. When she looked at him with those same terrified eyes he'd looked into when he'd opened his door to her, he knew she needed his help. And patience. "I'll start you off," he said. "What's this little guy's name?"

At the reference to her son, Amy seemed to light up a little.

Studying her, Connor could see a little of the old Amy struggling to surface.

"Jamie," she said, uttering the name almost reverently, as if the baby was the only thing still tethering her to life.

"How old is Jamie?" Connor asked, looking down into the cradle. After returning with tea for Amy, he'd begun gently rocking the boy again. Jamie looked as if he was about to drift off to sleep.

"He just turned six months," Amy answered fondly.

For the first time, Connor detected a note of pride in her voice. It was easy to see that whatever else was wrong in her life, the baby was clearly the center of her universe.

"Is he Clay's?" Connor asked.

At the mention of the other man's name, anger flashed across Amy's face. "He's *mine*," she said fiercely.

"And Clay's?" Connor prodded, his question technically still unanswered.

In the five years that Amy had been gone from Forever, the possibility that she had taken up with another man was definitely there. But he knew Amy, knew her like he knew his siblings and himself. Possibly even better. Amy wasn't the type to go from one man to another. She'd left town with Clay and he was willing to bet that she had remained with Clay—until something had forced her to flee with her baby.

"Yes," Amy admitted with a great deal of reluctance. The next moment she looked up at Connor and cried, "Oh, Connor, I've been such an idiot."

"We've all been there," he said, doing his best to get her to go easy on herself.

But it was obvious that she wasn't about to do that. "Not like me."

He'd never heard her sound so terribly sad before. "Why don't we talk about that later?" Changing the subject, Connor asked, "When was the last time you ate?"

Amy started to answer, then stopped. She thought for a moment and then, unable to remember, she shook her head, embarrassed.

"I don't know."

"Well, that ends now," he informed her. Taking charge—he didn't know how to do anything else—he rose to his feet. "You stay here and I'll put something together for you to eat."

He was already beginning to leave the living room to make good on his promise.

Amy looked at him in surprise. "You cook?"

Connor grinned. "Yeah, but I reheat better." And then he explained. "My housekeeper, Rita, went to visit her sister in Austin for a few days, but, bless her, she prepared a bunch of casseroles for me before she left. I think she was secretly afraid that I'd wind up subsisting on scrambled eggs three times a day until she got back."

This, too, was news to Amy. It made her realize even further that a great deal had happened since she had left Forever.

"You have a housekeeper?" she asked in amazement.

"That's right. You'd left town before Rita came to work for us."

He watched as Amy flushed at the mention of her having left town. Connor silently upbraided himself for having so carelessly tossed the phrase around. He didn't want to rub salt into her wounds, especially since he had no way of knowing what those wounds were or just how deep they actually went.

Wanting to distract her, Connor said, "Tell you what. Why don't you come into the kitchen with me? That way you can talk while I warm up your meal." He saw the reluctant expression on her face as Amy glanced toward the cradle. "Don't worry. If Jamie starts to cry, we'll hear him," Connor assured her. "The kitchen's only a few feet away."

It was all the persuasion she needed to sway her. Although still a little hesitant, Amy rose to her feet and followed Connor into the kitchen.

"When you said your housekeeper came to work for you, you used the word *us*," Amy began.

Opening the refrigerator door, he rummaged around.

There were still a number of casseroles to choose from, and Rita, bless her, had labeled everything.

"Yeah, I did," he answered absently.

"By 'us,' did you mean your brothers and Cassidy?" Amy asked.

"Yes," he told her, making his selection. He seemed to recall that turkey was always her favorite. But wanting to be sure he wasn't mistaken, he asked, "Turkey okay with you?"

"Anything is fine," she answered, although her smile told him that he had remembered correctly. He took the casserole out and shut the refrigerator again. "So where is everyone?" Amy wanted to know. Then, not wanting to seem as if she was digging into his personal life, she clarified by saying, "Cody, Cole and Cassidy. Are they out?"

Connor laughed softly. "Oh, they're out, all right. They're all out on their own." When he saw the slightly quizzical look on her face, he added, "As in married with kids."

"Really?" Although her own life had taken that course, somehow, she hadn't thought of anyone she'd left behind doing that. To discover otherwise was extremely eye-opening.

"Really. All three of them are married. They still live around here and Cole turns up like clockwork five mornings a week to help me with the work on the ranch," he said. He placed the casserole in the microwave oven and set the timer. "And everyone turns up here on Sundays for dinner. They'd all love to see you."

Just then, the microwave dinged, signaling that the

meal was warm enough, and he opened the door. Taking a towel, he carefully eased the hot dish out onto the counter.

"I doubt that," she murmured, almost more to herself than to him.

He looked up at her sharply.

"I don't," he countered. "And with Jamie by your side," he went on as he set the individual casserole dish right in front of her on the kitchen table, "you'd fit right in here."

The words were no sooner out of his mouth than he saw they had generated tears in her eyes.

"I really doubt that," she repeated in an even quieter voice.

Seeing her cry really got to him. He had always felt helpless in the presence of a woman's tears. The two times he'd been around Cassidy when she'd cried, he'd felt utterly at a loss, and Cassidy had never been one of those gentle little flowers despite the fact she was small in comparison to the rest of them.

But seeing Amy cry just ripped his insides to shreds—and even though he was by and large a nonviolent man at heart, it made Connor want to punch out whoever was the cause behind her tears.

Most likely, his number one candidate was Clay Patton, Connor thought. There'd never been any love lost between them to begin with and even less now.

Connor fisted his hands at his sides in mute frustration.

## Chapter Three

Sitting down at the table opposite Amy, Connor said nothing for a moment, letting her eat in peace. But good intentions notwithstanding, Connor could only remain quiet for so long.

Questions grew and burned on his tongue, seeking release. He contained them for as long as he could. While he respected Amy's privacy, there was a very strong need to know.

"Amy," he began, finally deciding to broach the subject, "I know that it's really none of my business, but what happened?"

Amy took a deep breath as if centering herself. It was obvious that she was doing her best to keep any more tears at bay.

"I guess I do owe you an explanation, turning up on your doorstep like this," she said.

"You don't 'owe' me an explanation," Connor told her gently. "You don't owe me anything, Amy. But if there's something that you want to talk about, something you need to get off your chest, then I'm here for you. To help, not to judge," he added, sensing that Amy might be afraid he would wind up looking down at her.

She didn't need that right now. Who would? What she needed was to feel safe and to know that someone was on her side, no strings attached. Amy had the same look in her eyes that one of the stray horses he'd found last summer had. There was only one thing that could put that look there: mistreatment.

But he wasn't about to make any assumptions or jump to conclusions. Whatever the story was, he needed to hear it from Amy.

As Connor paused, he saw Amy put her fork down even though she had barely touched her casserole.

Looking from the casserole to her face, Connor told her, "I can get you something else if you didn't find that to your liking."

"No, the casserole's very good," she quickly assured him, then said, "I just kind of lost my appetite."

"I'm sorry," he apologized. "That's my doing."

Connor felt bad. Instead of distracting her, he'd forced Amy to think about what had caused her to leave everything behind and come here.

"No, it's not," Amy insisted. "You've never been anything but kind to me." She paused, searching for words that seemed to be eluding her. And then she raised her eyes to his, fresh tears shimmering in hers. "He threw me out, Connor," she whispered haltingly. "Clay threw me out. He said some hateful words, telling me that I ruined his life, that Jamie and I were just lead weight dragging him down and he wanted us gone." She made a visible attempt to rally. "He was drunk at the time, but what he said still hurt."

Her voice was hollow as she continued. "When he passed out, I threw some things into a suitcase, took the baby and left." Amy stopped for a moment because her voice was close to breaking. Regaining control, she told him, "I didn't know where to go, so I just kept driving until I drove back down here."

He knew that her father had died eight years ago and her mother had remarried, eventually relocating out of state. An only child, Amy had no one to turn to.

Even if she did, he would have still made the offer he was making now. "You can stay here for as long as you need to," he told her with quiet sincerity. "For as long as you want."

But Amy shook her head. "I can't put you out like that."

"Who said anything about putting me out?" he asked. "You're not exactly twisting my arm here, Amy. Last I checked, I was able to make up my own mind and my mind's made up. You're staying here until you pull yourself together and figure out what it is that you want to do."

A wave of despair washed over her. It was hard not to drown in it. "What if I never figure out what I want to do?" she asked.

That was just the fear talking, Connor thought. What Amy needed right now was some reassurance—and some time to build up her self-esteem.

He smiled at her. "Then you and Jamie will just go on staying here. My dad built this house with his own hands and he made sure that there were plenty of bedrooms. He always said he might never have a lot of money, but he firmly believed it was having a family that made a man rich. Before Mom died, he really wanted to fill up all the rooms with kids."

Amy smiled. "I remember your dad. He was a really nice man."

"That he was," Connor agreed with a touch of wistfulness. And then his tone changed. "And he would have been all over my case for not making you eat your supper."

She looked down at the casserole. She had to admit that it *was* good. It was just that her stomach was tied up in knots. "Maybe, in honor of your dad, I should try to eat a little more."

Connor readily concurred. "Maybe you should."

The wail of a waking baby broke into his words. Amy was instantly alert.

"Jamie's awake," she said, pushing her chair back from the table.

Connor put his hand over hers on the table, holding her in place.

"You finish your supper. I'll see to the baby." He saw the uncertain expression on Amy's face. "Don't look so surprised. Thanks to Cody, Cole and Cassidy, I've really gotten to know my way around babies." On his feet, he pointed at the casserole dish before her. "Eat," he ordered as he turned on his heel and went to see why Jamie was crying.

Amy debated getting up and hurrying after him. She knew he'd told her that he could handle it, but Jamie was her son and she felt guilty about not tending to him. For the last six months, ever since Jamie had been born, hers was the only touch the baby had known. Clay had had absolutely no interest in holding his son, much less in doing any of the things that were involved in caring for the baby.

*He's your whelp. You take care of him*, Clay had snapped at her on the day that she came home from the hospital with Jamie. He hadn't even made the effort to bring her home. A neighbor had wound up being the one to do it.

It was the same neighbor who had taken her *to* the hospital when she'd gone into labor. Clay had been out and unavailable when her water broke. Her calls to him had gone straight to voice mail. Since he had next to no interest in holding down a job and was perpetually "between positions," as he liked to say, she could only guess that he was either out drinking with his friends, or out with one of the scores of women who were always pursuing him.

In these last six months, Clay's attitude toward Jamie never changed. It was indifference balanced out with anger. The anger especially flared up when Jamie's cries would interfere with his sleep, or with whatever program he was watching on TV.

Since Clay claimed not to be able to find any work he deemed suitable and she had been forced to leave her waitressing job when Jamie was born, all three of them were living off her savings and the money that her father had left her.

But between the bills—and Clay's gambling debts—that money was all but gone.

Worried sick and close to her wit's end, when Clay threw her out, she didn't bother to try to reconcile with him. Her gut told her it was time to leave. She realized there was always an outside chance that Clay would change his mind and tell her to stay. After all, she was his only source of income and he'd been pressuring her to go back to work. But after some soul-searching, she knew she couldn't stay with Clay any longer.

She didn't just have herself to think of anymore and there was no doubt in her mind that Clay Patton was not a good role model for Jamie, even though he was the boy's father. Moreover, she didn't want Jamie to grow up thinking that drinking, gambling and cheating on the woman he was married to were what a real man did.

But neither was running away, she told herself ruefully. That definitely wasn't the right example to set for Jamie, either.

Another tear slid down her cheek as she sat at the table, trying to sort things out.

When had life gotten to be so complicated?

As she wiped away the tear with the back of her hand, Amy realized the baby had stopped crying. The first thing that occurred to her was something was wrong. Jamie never stopped crying so quickly. Getting up, she hurried from the kitchen back to the living room.

She found Connor sitting on the sofa, holding her son and gently rocking him in his arms.

"Looks like your mom's come to check up on us,

Jamie," he told the baby. "I don't think she really trusts me with you yet."

Amy couldn't get over how peaceful Jamie seemed.

"It's not that I don't trust you, Connor," she began, not really knowing how to end her sentence without sounding as if she was a paranoid parent.

Taking pity on her, Connor bailed her out. "You're really not used to anyone taking care of Jamie but you, right?"

"Right. Clay's not good with babies—with Jamie," she explained.

Connor knew that he should just leave the comment alone. But the truth of it was, he had never liked Clay Patton, even back when they were all going to school together. The dislike had come very close to hatred when Clay had run off with Amy.

Which was undoubtedly why he heard himself saying, "Clay's not good with a lot of things," even though he knew he should just let the whole thing pass without making any sort of further comment.

"For the record," Connor went on, his voice softening, "I changed Jamie and I think that he might be getting hungry. He's trying to eat his fist. I've got some extra baby bottles, but I'm afraid there's no formula in the house. If you tell me what kind he needs, I'll go into town and get some for you."

"I've got formula," she said. It was one of the few things she'd made sure to pack, along with Jamie's things. Her son's needs came first, even when her brain had been in a state of turmoil.

She looked at Connor, some of his words replaying

themselves in her head. He'd changed Jamie, but she knew she hadn't given him any diapers. Those were still in her bag. Curiosity got the better of her.

"How did you get so—prepared?" she asked him.

"I can't take the credit for that. Cole's twins are less than a year old, so there are a few things that are still left over from when he first brought them to the house." He decided to give her a more concise picture of the way things had gone here in the last eighteen months. "When Cody first brought Devon and *her* baby to stay here, Miss Joan threw them a baby shower. Most of the things we still have here are from that shower, although some of them were acquired for Cassidy's castaway," he added.

"Her castaway," Amy repeated.

"The baby she rescued from the river," Connor elaborated.

Amy held up her hand. "Wait. My head's starting to hurt." She looked at him, clearly confused. She hadn't really been listening to Connor earlier when he'd given her a quick summary on his siblings. Her mind had been preoccupied with what she'd done and needed to do.

Listening to him now, it sounded to her as if each of his siblings had not just gotten married in a short amount of time, but had acquired babies, as well. It didn't seem probable.

"Are you pulling my leg?" she asked him.

"Why would I do that?" he asked.

Amy shrugged, at a loss as to how to explain her bewilderment. "I don't know. I guess because this all sounds a little fantastic."

Connor grinned at her, then glanced down at the baby in his arms—now sound asleep.

"You have a point," he agreed, then added, "But it's the truth. Since you're going to be staying here awhile, you'll get to see this for yourself. All of them will be here for Sunday dinner."

He had his family coming together on Sundays, she thought. She'd only be in the way. "I'll be imposing," she protested.

"No," he told her firmly, "you'll be here." There was no room for argument in his voice. "Now stop trying to argue with me or you'll wind up waking up your son and I just got him to sleep."

Amy shook her head, her eyes misting again. "I don't deserve you, Connor." She lightly brushed her lips against his cheek.

"What you don't deserve," he told her, doing his best not to react to the fleeting kiss and the warm glow it created within him, "is what happened to you before. But that's all in the past now." He spoke softly so as not to wake Jamie. "Like my dad used to like to say, today is the first day of the rest of your life. Doesn't matter what happened before. What matters is what you do with now—and what you do with tomorrow."

"You really mean it?" she asked, as if Connor's words were suddenly beginning to sink in. "I can stay here for now?"

He noticed that some of her color was finally beginning to come back to her cheeks. She didn't seem quite as stricken as she had when she'd first walked in.

"For now. And for much longer than that," he answered. "I can do it with hand puppets if you'd like, if it gets the message across to you any better."

Connor with hand puppets. She laughed at the image that created in her head. "No, that's not necessary. Message received, thank you."

"No," Connor contradicted, "thank *you*. The house was getting quieter than a tomb just before you got here. *Disturbingly* quiet," he emphasized. "Even when Rita's here, it's still eerily quiet. Rita's not exactly given to chattering endlessly.

"After growing up in a house full of siblings, usually with them arguing over something, all this peace and quiet is really getting on my nerves. I was thinking about getting a dog just before you got here. A yappy dog."

Amy visibly brightened at the idea of a four-legged pet running around. "I always wanted a dog," she confessed. "But my parents always said they were too much trouble. And I won't tell you what Clay had to say about getting a dog."

Connor frowned at the mention of Amy's estranged husband. "I'm guessing probably the same thing he had to say about having a baby."

She looked surprised that he had hit the nail right on the head the way he had.

"Yes," she admitted ruefully. "He did." She looked down at her sleeping son. "If it had been up to Clay, Jamie wouldn't be here—and there would have been this huge, awful gaping hole in my heart."

"Well, good thing for your heart he's here," Connor said in a cheerful voice, deliberately steering her away from the somber subject to something lighter. "Now why don't you go back to your supper and finish eating it while I take care of Jamie? You need to build up your strength."

"How did you know I didn't finish eating?" she asked in surprise.

"Because I'm the oldest in my family and I know everything," he said simply. "Now go and finish your supper—or there'll be no dessert."

He was rewarded with a soft laugh as Amy turned away to go back to the kitchen and her supper.

"Don't worry, Jamie," he whispered to the sleeping baby in his arms. "Your mom's going to be all right. We're going to take care of her, you and I."

Jamie made a little noise, as if in response, but went on sleeping.

## Chapter Four

This was more like it, Connor thought later that evening, after he'd cleared away the dishes and then come back into the living room to keep Amy and her son company. Although there certainly wasn't much of a commotion, he found the little sounds of ongoing life extremely comforting.

He swiftly began to realize that he wasn't meant for the solitary life. Amy and her son had appeared just in time. She might think that he was rendering her a service, taking her in this way, but the way he saw it, she was actually saving him. Saving him from a life of soul-draining desolation.

"Why don't you and Jamie spend the night in the guest bedroom down here for tonight?" Connor suggested when it came time to call it an evening. "I'll move the cradle in next to the bed, and then tomorrow I can get the crib out of the attic and set it up next to the guest bedroom upstairs." He smiled as he remembered each of the babies taking their turn sleeping in that room. "It seems to be the go-to bedroom for all our infant guests.

And if we leave the cradle down here, you can keep Jamie close by during the daytime."

The man had obviously thought of everything, Amy realized. She was more than a little gratified as she walked into the guest room. He was right behind her, bringing in the cradle.

She had no idea how to begin to thank him.

"You really are a very good man, Connor," she told him.

Connor saw no reason to take undue credit. The way he saw it, he hadn't done anything that was out of the ordinary. "It's family, Amy. You do what you have to do for family."

"But I'm not your family," she pointed out.

Connor shrugged. "A technicality."

Amy's smile turned sad around the edges as she said, "Not everyone feels that way."

He could tell she was thinking about Clay, and although he wanted to tell her the man wasn't worth a single one of her tears or even a moment's worth of regret, Connor knew it wasn't his place to say that to her. For all he knew, she still loved Clay and she was still married to the man.

With that in mind, he tried to be supportive. "He might still come looking for you, you know."

Oh Lord, with all her heart, she hoped not.

"If he does, it's not because he loves me. That ship sailed a long time ago. If he does come looking for me, it's only because he thinks of me as his property and his ego can't abide the thought that I'd actually leave him."

"But he threw you out," he reminded Amy.

She shook her head, overruling his point. "That doesn't matter. He threw me out, but I think that in Clay's mind I should be begging him to take me back."

And that brought them to the major question that had been nagging at him since she'd walked in. "And do you want him to?"

Amy's answer was quick and emphatic. "No! I've done my penance," she told Connor with feeling. "And I've finally come to my senses."

The smile that curved his mouth was a reflection of the warmth he was feeling inside. "Glad to hear that," he said with enthusiasm. Then, not to appear as if he was dwelling on what she'd just said, he turned to a more practical subject. "I brought you new linens and some fresh towels." He pointed to both piles he'd placed on the bureau earlier. "If there's anything else you can think of that you might need, all you have to do is ask. I can bed down here on the couch," he offered, "so I can be close by if you decide that you *do* need something."

But she wasn't about to hear of him having to spend the night on the sofa because of her. "I've already put you out enough as it is and I've got everything I need right here."

He didn't want her to feel as if he was putting any undue pressure on her and he would be the first to acknowledge how important it was to retain a sense of independence.

"All right," he said as he headed toward the door, "then I guess I'll say good-night and turn in."

Connor was almost at the threshold when he heard her call after him.

"Connor?"

He turned around quickly, thinking that she had remembered something she needed. "Yes?"

Gratitude was shining in her eyes as she said, "Thank you."

The two words caused sunshine to filter all through him. He hadn't felt like that since they were kids in high school.

"My pleasure," he told her.

The next moment he pulled the door closed behind him and then he was gone.

Amy stood in the small, homey guest room for a long time, just looking at the closed door. A peaceful feeling sank in by small increments. She was safe. For the first time in a very long time, she was safe.

"Well, we did it, Jamie," she whispered softly to the child, who was asleep in the nearby cradle. "We escaped. Now all we have to do is figure out what to do with the rest of our lives."

She sighed as she sank down on the double bed. "Tomorrow," she said, her voice still a soft whisper. "I'll figure it out tomorrow."

Amy was convinced she wouldn't get much sleep, given the amount of extra tension she'd experienced by finally getting up the nerve to pick up and leave. But it was exactly that tension—and the accumulated tension from the last five years—that had her so exhausted. She was asleep before her head even hit the oversize pillow Connor had placed on her bed.

CONNOR FELT LIKE hell when he came downstairs the next morning. If he'd gotten an hour's worth of sleep, spread out across the last six, he had done well.

For the most part, he'd lain awake, listening for any sounds that were out of the ordinary. Mainly, he had been listening for Amy calling him in the middle of the night. Twice he'd gotten up and stood on the landing of the stairs, straining his ears and listening in case he'd somehow missed hearing her.

But other than the sound of a coyote howling in the distance, there was nothing to break up the silence.

Even Amy's baby was silent, which, compared to the other four infants who had spent time at the ranch, was highly unusual.

But Connor went on listening just in case, which explained why he felt as if he'd been run over by a stampeding herd of mustangs when he came down the following morning.

Struggling to focus his eyes, he stumbled into the kitchen, intent on making himself a strong cup of coffee and hopefully jump-starting his system.

It was his heart that underwent the jump start when he almost walked right into all five-foot-one of the moving dynamo who was his housekeeper.

"Rita," he exclaimed, startled. "You're back." Still feeling out of focus, he struggled to clear his head. "Weren't you supposed to get back next Monday?" he asked the woman.

"Yes," Rita answered, clearing off the counter as she prepared to make breakfast, "but I decided to come back early and I see that I was right to cut my visit to my sister short." Rita had never been one to mince words. "You look like hell, Mr. Connor." She eyed him suspiciously. "You have not been eating your own cooking, have you? I know that I prepared enough meals for you to last until I returned."

"My cooking's not that bad," Connor protested.

Rita took his protest to mean that the rancher had been cooking. She frowned. "Then you *have* been eating your own meals."

"No, Rita," Connor responded dutifully, "I've been eating your casseroles, just like you told me."

Still eyeing him suspiciously, Rita fisted her hands on her waist. Something was definitely off. "Then why do you look like that?"

Connor went with a simple answer first, hoping it would be enough to satisfy the woman. "I didn't get any sleep last night."

Concern instantly washed over the older woman's face. "Is there something wrong? Did someone in the family get sick?" she asked. "Who is it? I will go right over there—"

"Calm down, Rita. Nobody's sick." He caught the woman by her sturdy shoulders, holding her in place, although it wasn't all that easy.

Her attention circled back to him and she gave him a dubious look. "Have you taken a look at yourself in the mirror this morning?"

"I appreciate your concern, Rita. I do," he said patiently. "But I'd appreciate a cup of coffee even more."

Rita sighed. She was accustomed to the rancher's

slow, stubborn behavior. He was not one to volunteer information quickly.

"Very well, Mr. Connor. I will make you your coffee," Rita said. Taking the coffeepot, she measured out three cups of water and then placed the required amount of coffee grounds into the coffee machine.

"And make a couple of extra cups this morning," he requested.

Rita stopped and added water to the pot and measured out more coffee grounds to accommodate his request. "Mr. Cole coming early?"

"No, he's coming the usual time," Connor answered. Opening the refrigerator, he rummaged through the different shelves. He didn't find what he was looking for. "Rita, do we have any more jam?"

"In the pantry." The coffee maker began to go through its paces, making noises as it brewed. Rita turned to look at him. "Since when do you take jam?" she wanted to know. Before he could answer her, the distant sound of a baby crying had Rita looking alert. "Am I hearing a baby cry?"

"I don't know," he deadpanned. "Are you?"

She listened more closely. "That sounds too young to belong to Mr. Cole's twins."

"Good ear," Connor complimented, deftly avoiding what he knew the woman was ultimately after. "Listen, why don't I just pour the coffee and get the jam and you just—"

Rita placed herself in front of the rancher, a small, formidable human roadblock. Her dark eyes narrowed as they delved into him.

"Another one?" she cried.

"Another what?" Connor asked innocently, deciding to draw the conversation out just a little bit and tease the housekeeper.

"I leave here for five days and you found another baby?" she asked, astonished. "That makes—five," she declared after doing a quick review in her head. "A total of five babies. It is like your whole family are baby magnets."

"Technically," Connor corrected, "the baby found me. Or actually the baby's mother found me."

No longer needing to behave like a human blockade, Rita turned on her heel and headed directly toward the sound of the crying baby.

"Rita, wait up," Connor called after her. "I'll make the introductions after I—"

Since she had come to work for the McCulloughs, Rita had very quickly become not just part of the family but had taken on the role of a surrogate mother. She had no interest in waiting for any introductions to be made. If there were introductions to be made, she would be the one to take care of that small detail.

She continued to head for the rear guest bedroom like a homing pigeon on a mission. Stopping at the door only long enough to deliver a short, quick knock, she barely heard a woman's voice say "Come in" before she had her hand on the doorknob. The next moment, she'd opened the door and was walking in.

Amy looked up, startled. She'd expected to see Connor coming in. Instead, she found herself looking at a small, dark-haired matronly woman who looked as if she was accustomed to being in charge of anything and everything she came across.

Amy's hand flew to her chest as if to steady her pounding heart.

"I'm sorry—who are you?" she asked the woman who made no secret of swiftly dissecting her with her dark eyes.

"I am Rita Navarro," Rita informed her. "Who are you?"

Entering, Connor came between the two women, prepared to act as a human buffer. In his opinion, the housekeeper was a wonderful woman, but she had a tendency to come on too strong at times.

"Amy, this is my housekeeper, Rita. She tends to think she runs everything."

Rita spared him a quick side glance. "That is because I do." She pressed her thin lips together as she shook her head. "This will teach me to go away," she murmured under her breath, scrutinizing the young woman sitting on the bed, holding the baby in her arms.

There was only one way for her to interpret the older woman's comment. "Then I am intruding," Amy said, rising to her feet. "I'll go," she told Connor.

"No, you're not, and no, you won't," Connor replied firmly. He gave Rita a warning glance over his shoulder, silently telling the woman to weigh her words.

Rita tempered her tone as she asked Amy, "How old is your baby?"

"He's six months old," Amy answered. She still looked as if she was somewhat intimidated by the petite but bombastic housekeeper.

Rita nodded, as if the information jibed with something in her head.

"Bring him to the kitchen. When I finish preparing your breakfast, I will take care of him while you eat. Come," she ordered the baby's mother just before she left the room.

"And that," Connor cavalierly said to Amy, "is my housekeeper. I should have warned you—she comes on a little strong."

A small smile curved the corners of Amy's mouth. "*Strong.* That would be the word for it, all right," she agreed.

"Rita means well," Connor assured her.

She could only hope that was true, Amy thought, but out loud she said, "I'm sure she does."

"Are you coming?" Rita called out from the kitchen.

"I think we've just been given our marching orders," Connor said, about to take Amy's elbow to usher her and the baby into the kitchen. "For a small woman, her voice can really carry," he observed with a laugh. And then, thinking that perhaps the housekeeper's overbearing manner might be rather difficult for Amy to deal with, he said, "I can talk to Rita and ask her to back off."

But Amy shook her head. She did not want to risk possibly getting on the woman's bad side. "That's okay. She's just looking out for you."

"Stay here a day and she'll be looking out for you, as well," Connor promised. "She might seem gruff, but she's really good with kids."

"Right now, I'll settle for her just being good with coffee," Amy said.

"You're about to have your wish come true." He could smell the coffee brewing even before he crossed the threshold to the kitchen.

"Ah, so you are finally here," Rita declared. Her back was to them. It was as if she could sense their presence. "Good. The coffee is ready and so is your breakfast." She nodded at the two place settings on the table, then turned around and crossed to Amy. "Here, give him to me."

"That's all right. I can hold him while I eat," Amy said.

"But you can eat better if I hold him," Rita informed her in a firm voice. Putting out her hands, she waited for the baby to be transferred to her. "Do not worry. I do not drop children."

Feeling somewhat uneasy, Amy surrendered Jamie to the housekeeper. The moment that she did, she watched in fascination as a smile blossomed on the woman's otherwise stern face, instantly transforming her.

Rita began cooing something to the baby in Spanish, and then she looked up, sparing Amy a glance. "Eat before it gets cold," she ordered.

"You heard the lady." Connor ushered Amy into a chair. "Breakfast is a lot better warm—and so is Rita," he added with a whisper.

Amy suppressed a laugh as she sat down, feeling a little more at ease. Maybe, she thought, she'd been right to come here after all.

## Chapter Five

"Hey, Connor, whose car is that parked out in front of the house?" Cole McCullough asked as he made his way through the living room into the kitchen.

The second-oldest McCullough brother stopped dead when he saw the answer to his question sitting at the kitchen table, having breakfast across from his brother.

"Amy?" Cole said uncertainly.

Not quite sure how he would react to seeing her there with Connor, Amy forced a smile to her lips as she greeted Connor's brother.

"Hello, Cole. How are you?" she asked politely.

Stunned, Cole blinked. Connor didn't usually have company. Certainly not at this hour in the morning and certainly not someone who had eloped five years ago. He half expected her to disappear.

But she didn't.

"I'm great," he told her, then repeated, "Just great."

Cole had no idea what to say to the woman he knew had left town with Connor's heart unwittingly packed away in her suitcase. Connor never talked about it, but he didn't have to. He, Cody and Cassidy all knew how

Connor felt about Amy. How he'd felt about her ever since they were kids. Although he had devoted himself to raising them and keeping the ranch going, they all knew that Connor was in love with Amy.

But because of them and all his obligations, Connor never had a chance to act on it. And then Clay Patton had set his sights on her, scooped her up and left town. Cole, like the rest of his family, just assumed that the story had ended there.

Apparently not, he thought, looking at Amy.

Cole finally got back the use of his tongue. "Are you here for a visit?" he asked her. He glanced at Connor for help. He needed to be bailed out before he wound up unintentionally putting his foot in his mouth.

"Amy's considering moving back to Forever," Connor replied quietly, deliberately keeping the situation open-ended for her.

"You are here just in time, Mr. Cole," Rita announced as she came into the kitchen, holding Amy's son in her capable arms.

Surprised to see that the housekeeper had returned early, Cole was even more surprised to see that Rita was holding a baby in her arms and feeding that same baby with a bottle.

"Welcome back, Rita," Cole said, greeting the woman. "I take it that you don't mean I'm just in time for breakfast, do you?"

Impatience creased the woman's already furrowed brow. "You can have some coffee if you wish and then you can help Mr. Connor bring down the crib from the attic."

"The one we just put back up there a couple of months ago?" he asked, looking quizzically at Connor.

It felt as if that crib, used for each of the babies who had been here—not to mention that it had once been Cassidy's when she was a baby—had more mileage on it than his truck did.

"That would be the one," Connor confirmed. "And it was closer to almost four months ago," he reminded his brother. "That was when you and Stacy moved into the old McNally place and bought the twins separate cribs of their own."

Amy still couldn't picture Cole as a father, much less as the father of two. "You have twins?" she asked him.

But Cole appeared more interested in what was going on at the moment than history, especially his own past.

"I take it that's your baby," he said, nodding at the baby the housekeeper was holding.

"You found out my secret, Mr. Cole," Rita said, her solemn expression remaining unchanged. "I was jealous of all of you with your babies, so I decided to have one of my own."

She looked so perfectly serious, for a moment Cole didn't know if the housekeeper was joking or if the woman had actually made off with someone's baby for some reason she had yet to reveal.

Cole glanced at his brother again. "She's kidding, right?"

"Yes, genius, she's kidding," Connor said. "The baby belongs to Amy and Amy will be staying here for a while." He glanced in her direction, secretly waiting for her contradiction.

"Just until I figure out what I'm going to do," Amy added quickly. She didn't want to come across like a mooch. "Connor was nice enough to put us up."

"Hey, you don't have to explain anything to me. I'm the one who came home with twins one morning," he told Amy with a laugh.

She was still trying to sort that all out. There'd been a great deal of information flying at her since she'd walked in yesterday. "Then the twins you mentioned aren't yours?"

"Well," Cole said, "they are now because we adopted them."

"'We'?" Confused, Amy looked at Connor, for some reason thinking Cole was referring to his brother and himself when he used the pronoun.

"He means Stacy," Connor explained.

"Stacy and I got married," Cole added in an attempt to lessen some of the confusion. "You remember Stacy Rowe from school, don't you? She came back to Forever."

"I didn't know she was gone," Amy confessed. It felt as if her head was spinning as she tried to sort out the information that was coming at her at what she felt was lightning speed.

"That's right," Cole recalled. "You'd already left town with—" Catching himself just in time, Connor's brother rephrased his statement. "You'd already left Forever before Stacy did."

Rita grunted, signaling an end to the present discussion. "Why don't you two let the poor girl finish her breakfast in peace?" Rita suggested forcefully. "You can use that extra energy of yours to get the crib down from the attic and bring it into the nursery," she told the two brothers, referring to the room next to the bedroom that Stacy had used before she had married Cole.

"Ah, I've missed those dulcet tones of yours these last few days," Cole told her as he walked by the house-keeper.

Rita's jet-black eyebrows narrowed as she fixed the younger man with a glare. "You are just lucky I am holding this baby, Mr. Cole, or I would box your ears."

"C'mon, Connor," Cole urged his brother. "Let's go get the crib before she puts that baby down and makes good on her threat."

"It is only a threat if I do not do it," Rita said, calling after the departing brothers.

Without missing a beat, the housekeeper turned around to focus her attention on Amy. Seeing that the ranch's newest houseguest had finished what was on her plate, Rita asked, "Would you like something more to eat?"

Thinking about what Cole had just said, Amy had been caught off guard by Rita's question. It took her a second to process it.

"Oh no, thank you," Amy quickly demurred. "I'm so full, if I had one more bite I might just explode. Every-thing was delicious," she added, not wanting to some-how offend the woman by forgetting to compliment her efforts.

"Everything was all right," Rita corrected. "Deli-cious will be served for dinner," she informed the young woman with the same straight face she had used to tell

Cole that the baby she was holding was her own. Then, giving Amy a penetrating look that seemed to somehow delve into her innermost thoughts, she told her, "It is all right to smile once in a while, Miss Amy. No one will think less of you for it."

Amy flushed. She didn't want to come off as some sort of a sourpuss, especially after she'd been taken in the way she had by Connor.

"I'm sorry. It's just…" Her voice trailed off as she tried to find the right way to say what she was feeling.

Rita seemed to be way ahead of her as she nodded knowingly.

"I know—it is hard to accept that things are not the way you thought they would be and that you need to take the help that is offered to you. But you are not the first to be in this position and you will not be the last. Now," she told Amy as she began to leave the kitchen, "have another cup of coffee while I go to change your son."

At the mention of changing Jamie, Amy was on her feet. "I'll do it."

Rita gave her a look that forbade her to move. "You will get more coffee and then you will sit and drink that coffee. I will change your son. You can change him the next time he needs it," she said by way of appeasing what she took to be the young woman's need to take care of her baby. "There will be many more opportunities for you to do it before he learns to take care of his own needs," Rita assured her as she left the kitchen.

Because she didn't want to make waves and cause any further discord, Amy sat down again and savored her second cup of coffee.

Then, taking advantage of the fact that the house-keeper had left the room and Connor was in the attic with Cole, she gathered up both her plate and Connor's, as well as the utensils they'd used, brought them all over to the sink and then quickly washed them.

It gave her a small sense of satisfaction to be useful, even in such a minor way.

She had just put everything on the rack to dry when Rita returned to the kitchen. Expecting a reprimand, she was surprised when the housekeeper smiled at her.

"You did not have to do that," Rita told her.

"I wanted to," Amy answered. "I don't like being lazy."

A small laugh escaped Rita's lips. "You are the mother of a six-month-old. *Lazy* is not a word that be-longs in your world. Here, take your son." Rita handed the baby over to her. "I have been gone five days and there are many things I need to organize and clean," she announced.

A thud coming from somewhere on the second floor had Rita glancing up toward the ceiling. "They have brought down the crib. Go and tell them where you want it."

"Won't they put it where they usually do?" Amy asked the housekeeper.

She doubted the two brothers would appreciate her ordering them around, especially since this was their ranch house and she was there only as Connor's guest. If anything, putting in her two cents seemed rather un-grateful to her.

"But that may not suit your needs and you are the

baby's mother. Now go, shoo," she added for good measure, waving Amy and her baby out of the kitchen.

"Yes, ma'am," Amy murmured as she quickly left the room.

Turning away, Rita smiled to herself.

"She is learning," she muttered under her breath, pleased.


"Did you come here to supervise?" Connor asked as Amy ventured into the room that he and his brother had just brought the crib into.

She didn't want Connor to think she was willfully trying to get in his way.

"It was Rita's idea," Amy said. "She told me to come upstairs to tell you where I wanted the crib."

"So where *do* you want it?" Connor asked. He and Cole had just brought the crib in, narrowly negotiating the doorway, which was only a little larger than the width of the crib.

"Anyplace," Cole panted, putting his end of the crib down.

Connor looked at his brother over his shoulder. "I was asking Amy."

"Wherever you had it before is fine," Amy said quickly. "Cole's face is red," she noted with concern.

Connor made a dismissive noise. "That's just for your benefit," he told her. "He wants you to think that he carried the brunt of the crib coming down the stairs."

"I did," Cole declared, wiping his brow with the back of his hand.

Connor looked at her and deadpanned, "Cole was actually the runt of the litter."

"Said the man who's looking to work the ranch alone for the rest of the month," Cole concluded, taking in a bracing breath.

Ignoring Connor, Amy shifted Jamie to her other side as she asked the other man, "Can I get you something to drink?"

"Don't encourage him," Connor said. "He'll just go on milking this for hours. He's actually as strong as an ox."

Cole gave him a dark look. "A minute ago I was the runt of the litter."

Connor shrugged, unfazed. "Even oxen have runts," he quipped.

"Nice save," Cole commented. "You just don't want to come off looking like a slave driver in front of Amy and have her thinking badly of you."

"I'd never think badly of Connor," Amy told Cole, coming to Connor's defense. "Your brother is one of the really good guys."

Cole laughed as he eyed his brother. "You sure we're talking about the same Connor McCullough?"

Amy smiled. She had no idea where she would have gone if she hadn't had Connor to turn to. "Very sure," she replied.

"Well, looks like you've got her fooled," Cole said to his brother.

"Shouldn't you be getting to work on the stable door?" Connor reminded him. That was the first chore on their list for today.

"Why?" Cole asked, pretending to still recover from bringing the crib down from the attic. The stairs leading from there to the second floor were steep. "It's not going anywhere."

"No, but the horses might if that door hinge gets any weaker," Connor pointed out. It was still in place, but it wouldn't take all that much for it to come loose.

"All right, all right," Cole said with a sigh. "Now that we've got the crib back in the nursery, I'll go see about that stable-door hinge." He paused for half a second just as he walked by Amy. "Like I said, a slave driver," he told her with a wink.

The give-and-take between the two brothers had left Amy smiling, as well as reminding her of just what she had missed out on by being an only child. It was obvious that the McCulloughs might squabble at times, but the love that was there between them was impossible to miss.

"Now that he's gone," Connor said, turning around to face her, "we can get back to fixing up this room. Would you like me to move the crib?"

Amy shook her head. She saw no reason to have to do anything. She liked the crib just where it was, in the center of the room. "No, where you have it is just fine," she told Connor.

"Well, if you change your mind, let me know," Connor said as he began to cross to the doorway. "I'd better get over to Cole before he starts telling everyone that I left him with all the work." About to leave, he saw the way Amy was chewing on her lower lip. "Something wrong, Amy?"

"No, just the opposite," she answered. Then, because her reply probably raised more questions for him, she said, "Cole seems okay with my being here."

"Sure. Why shouldn't he be?" he asked. Cole wouldn't have said anything to her to make her feel unwanted. This had to be something in her head.

"I was just worried that he might think I was taking advantage," she said.

"Of what? Hospitality?" he asked, confused. "That's free and it goes without saying." She should know that, he thought.

"No, of you," she said. Because he didn't look as if he understood, she tried to explain it better. "Of our, um, friendship. You are putting me up."

"Not a hardship," Connor assured her. "And this *is* one-quarter my house."

She supposed that was what was bothering her. "Doesn't that mean that the others have something to say about who you take in?"

"They do," he agreed. "And the word they would say is 'yes.'"

He was just being kind and she didn't want to be the cause of any family discord. She still wasn't convinced that the others would welcome her being there, even if they all had their own homes now.

"But—"

"Amy, you're overthinking this," he told her. He saw her opening her mouth and he anticipated that she'd raise more nonexistent objections. "Stop thinking," he ordered with a smile. "Now see if your son likes his new sleeping arrangements—" he nodded at the infant in her arms "—and I'll see you later."

"Later," Amy murmured, watching him walk out.

She had to admit, the word had a definite good feel about it.

## Chapter Six

It was a full week before Connor was finally able to make a trip into town. In that time, Rita had made two trips to the general store for food, but between his trying to be there for Amy to help her acclimate to her new life and keeping the ranch running and productive, Connor had just been too busy to make the trip to Forever himself.

His list of things he needed kept growing until he couldn't put off going to town any longer, so he went one morning right after breakfast.

Once he'd picked up everything he needed from the general store, as well as from its adjacent hardware store, Connor allowed himself a few minutes of luxury by making a quick stop at Miss Joan's Diner.

The diner, with its redheaded firecracker of an owner, was thought by one and all to be the very center of Forever, even though logistically it was a little right of the center of town. But perfectly centered or not, the diner—and Miss Joan—was considered to be the veritable heartbeat of the town.

When his father had died and he had been faced with

trying to provide for his siblings, as well as keeping the ranch from going under and being taken over by the bank, it was Miss Joan who had supplied his family and him with more than a few hot meals. And when money was particularly tight, the woman found part-time jobs for them and placed them on her payroll for however long it took to get the struggling family back on their feet.

And somehow, she managed to do it all without making it feel like charity. With her whiskey voice and her sharp, abrupt manner, she made them feel as if they were working for everything they received.

Throughout it all, with all she had to do, Miss Joan still made sure they never did without. Over time, he and his brothers and sister had all come to regard her as a surrogate mother. Surly, but nonetheless loving in the ways that counted.

Mindful of the fact that he had to be getting back soon, Connor walked up to the counter and planted himself on a stool.

"Morning, Miss Joan," he said as she turned around to make eye contact with him. "I'll have a cup of your strongest coffee, please."

To his surprise, Miss Joan said nothing in response to his greeting or his request. Instead, the woman silently poured a cup of coffee from the urn and then placed it right in front of him.

Still silent, she stood on the other side of the counter, studying him.

The woman had eyes like a laser, going right through him, Connor thought.

"Something wrong, Miss Joan?" Connor asked, keeping his voice mild.

Rather than answer his question, Miss Joan made an observation. "You know, I never thought of you as being the strong, silent type."

"I never thought of you that way, either," Connor responded, doing his best to keep a straight face as he lobbed the ball back into her court.

Connor had no idea why Miss Joan had said that or where this was going. He'd only been gone a week, he thought. Things couldn't have changed that much in one week. If anything major had taken place in Forever, or with Miss Joan, he was fairly confident that one of his brothers or Cassidy would have mentioned it to him over the course of the week.

Miss Joan's penetrating hazel-green eyes narrowed as she pinned him with a look. "Very funny, boy." Letting out an exasperated sigh, she became more blunt. "When were you going to tell me?"

About to raise his cup to his lips for another long, bracing sip of the pitch-black brew, he paused to look at her, utterly confused.

"I'm sorry?"

"Well, I should hope so," Miss Joan retorted. "But that still doesn't answer my question." Her lips pursed as she waited for a response. When she didn't get one, Miss Joan shook her head and then slowly enunciated each word of her question. "When were you going to tell me that Amy was back in town?"

It was an oversight, he silently admitted, but it hadn't been done deliberately. Now that he understood what was bothering her, he found a way to technically bail himself out and remain in her good graces.

"I didn't think I had to." He saw her thin lips deepen in a displeased frown. "You're Miss Joan—you know about things happening before they even happen."

"Flattery is not going to save you, boy."

He smiled at her gamely. "All right. What will?"

"I'll have to think on that," the woman informed him in a tone a judge used when deliberating over a prison sentence for a convicted offender. "In the meantime," she continued, her voice dripping with disapproval, "you can tell me if that girl finally came to her senses and left that no-account, flashy two-bit Romeo she ran off with."

"She did," Connor replied quietly, trying to keep the conversation just between the two of them despite the fact there were more than a few of the regular patrons in the diner.

Miss Joan snorted with approval. "Glad to hear that," she pronounced. "Did he ever bother to marry her?"

"Yes, ma'am," Connor answered even though it obviously pained him to say it.

"But she divorced him" were the next words out of her mouth. It wasn't so much of a question as an assumption.

"I'm not sure," Connor admitted. When Miss Joan looked at him sharply, he told the diner owner, "I didn't ask."

"Well, ask, boy," the woman ordered. "And if she hasn't, you see to it that she does, you hear me? Otherwise, there's going to be trouble," Miss Joan predicted.

"It's not my place to tell her to get a divorce if she didn't," Connor pointed out. Amy was her own woman, and as such, she was able to make her own decisions. And while he would have wanted nothing more than to have her free, he felt that in all good conscience, he couldn't tell Amy what to do one way or another.

Miss Joan obviously saw it differently. "Then whose place is it?" she asked. Before he could say anything to deflect her question or construct any sort of a defense, Miss Joan had leaned in closer and lowered her voice even more. "Sometimes, boy, you have to step in and help the people you care about even if they resist your efforts. Now go home and have that conversation with Amy. And then bring her by the next time you come into town. I'd like to see her. It's been a long time."

"Longer than you think," Connor commented under his breath, thinking of Jamie.

He should have realized that he was underestimating the older woman's ability to hear things.

"Oh," Miss Joan said by way of parting just before she made her way to another part of the counter and another customer who needed her attention, "and have her bring that baby of hers, too. We'll be doing our annual tree decorating in the center of Forever. Might do her good to feel like she's part of something again. The baby, too."

The woman never ceased to amaze him. "You *know* about the baby?"

Miss Joan paused only long enough to answer his question. "Of course I know about the baby. Like you said, I'm Miss Joan. I know everything, remember? Bring her." This time, it sounded more like a command.

One he should listen to because if anyone had the

ability to bring Amy around and set her on the right path, it was Miss Joan.

Connor had no doubt that when Amy left Clay, she'd had every intention of leaving him for good. But he also knew that time had a way of softening all the rough edges and burying the bad memories while highlighting the good ones. He was afraid that would happen in Amy and Clay's case. Especially if Amy was still married to the man.

Miss Joan was right, he thought as he climbed back into his truck. He needed to find out if Amy had gotten a divorce or if she was still married to Clay. While he would protect her with his dying breath if it came to that, he didn't relish the idea of coming between a husband and his wife.

Which was why, if she hadn't already, Amy needed to get a divorce.

ALL THE WAY home from Forever, Connor rehearsed what he was going to say to Amy. But the second he pulled up in front of his ranch house and turned off his truck's engine, the words he'd been going over became all jumbled up in his head.

This was definitely not going to be easy, he told himself as he got out of the reliable vehicle.

He'd gotten all the way up to the front door when he had to stop abruptly and double back to his truck. He realized that he'd left the supplies he'd gone into town to buy in his truck.

Or maybe he didn't forget, he thought. Maybe he was just trying to stall.

Either way, he knew he could only drag his feet for so long. He needed to ask Amy if she'd just left Clay, or if she'd divorced the man.

He crossed his fingers, hoping it was the latter.

Damn, he hated to feel like he was prying, Connor thought as he opened the front door and walked in, juggling bags of supplies. Putting everything down on the coffee table, he looked around.

He didn't see Rita, which was just as well. He wasn't up to being subjected to her questions and Rita *always* had questions when he came back from town.

At first, he didn't see Amy, either.

He thought she might be in the downstairs guest room, or maybe upstairs in her room. But the sound of splashing and Amy's laughter coming from the kitchen drew him there. Even though he didn't relish what he was about to ask, hearing Amy laugh brought a smile to his lips before he reached the kitchen.

He'd missed hearing her laugh. Missed, he admitted, everything about her.

He found Amy at the sink because she was bathing Jamie.

She had one of her arms underneath his little torso and the baby seemed to take exceptional delight in splashing up a storm. For a long moment, Connor just stood there, watching them and thinking how incomplete his life had seemed only a week ago. And now, taking in this scene, it felt amazingly full.

Knowing he couldn't continue just standing there indefinitely like some hidden observer, Connor finally spoke up.

"Need a hand?"

Amy gasped. Automatically pulling her baby against her, she turned to look over her shoulder. "Oh, Connor, you startled me."

"Sorry," he apologized, coming forward. "I can be pretty scary."

"No, I meant that I thought you weren't home. When I heard that deep voice, I thought—I thought—" Not wanting to finish her sentence and spoil the moment by saying that she'd thought Clay had caught up to her, she shrugged. "Never mind what I thought. Did you get everything in town you wanted?" she asked brightly, changing the subject.

He didn't want to talk about something so trivial as a shopping trip into town. The scared expression on her face had gotten to him.

"Never mind that right now. You looked frightened just then. If you thought I wasn't in the house, who *did* you think had just come in?" Connor asked, although he had his suspicions.

"It's not important," Amy told him, dismissing the subject. "Right now, I have to finish giving Jamie his bath."

"I'll help. And whatever's responsible for that terrified look on your face is very important," he stressed. "Level with me, Amy. Did you think it was Clay?"

"No," she denied quickly, and then, because she didn't want to lie to him, she amended, "Yes." Amy sighed. "Just for a second. But I'll get over it."

Since she'd come here with her son, she hadn't talked very much about Jamie's father. She'd given him the bare bones of the situation and he'd had to fill in the blanks. But this was about more than a woman leaving a man who cheated on her.

"Are you afraid that Clay is going to come looking for you?" he asked.

This was not a conversation she wanted to have. But then, she couldn't bring herself to lie to Connor, either. "I did tell you that he doesn't give up easily."

Connor thought of what Miss Joan had said to him earlier in the diner. "Amy, did you just leave Clay, or did you also divorce him?"

"Is that important?" Amy asked defensively, her eyes meeting his over the baby she was bathing. "I mean, to you?"

In the sum total of things, he didn't care. He was there for Amy and her son no matter what. But there was the legal aspect to consider—for her sake. "It's important because if he's your ex-husband, I can throw him out on his butt if he comes anywhere near you."

Did that mean the reverse was true, too? "But if he's still my husband, you can't?"

Connor patiently explained it to her. He didn't want to add to her burden by telling her that he loved her enough to walk through fire for her even if she *had* rejected him by running off with Clay. Instead, he focused on the facts.

"If he's still your husband, he could try to say I'm interfering in his marriage, but he's still not coming anywhere near you," Connor promised her. "I just need to know if you two are divorced or not."

"It's complicated," Amy confessed. "I didn't come

directly to you when I left Clay. I stayed in a motel for a couple of days and got in touch with a lawyer I found online. I filed for a divorce through him and he was supposed to send the papers to Clay. As far as I know, Clay still hasn't signed the papers—not because he cares about me or the baby, but because he just likes being controlling."

"Then we're going to have to take care of that," Connor said decisively. "As long as you still want to go through with it," he qualified. "I don't want to talk you into anything."

"You're not," she assured him. There were only so many excuses she could make for Clay before she had to face the truth. The man didn't love her; he never had. He'd just amused himself with her—until she ceased to be amusing. "Clay did that all on his own."

"Okay, then maybe you should make an appointment with either Olivia Santiago or Cash Taylor," Connor suggested, mentioning the town's only two lawyers, "and tell them about your situation. They'll help you."

"They're not divorce lawyers, are they?" Amy asked hopefully.

"They're lawyers," Connor said. "And since they're the only two in town, they handle pretty much everything. They'll look into getting the divorce finalized for you. Olivia's the sheriff's wife and Cash is Miss Joan's stepgrandson. You couldn't *be* in better hands to resolve this situation."

Amy smiled up at him. "I'm already in good hands," she told him.

"You still have that lawyer?" Connor asked.

"No, I think that maybe he just took advantage of my situation. But I have you," she told him. "And there's nobody that I trust in this whole wide world more than you."

"Then if you trust me, listen to me. We're going to make an appointment and go see Olivia or Cash—or both of them for good measure, and get this taken care of once and for all."

"Only one problem," she told him.

"What?" he asked guardedly.

"I can't pay them," Amy said. She'd barely had enough money for the gas it took to get here.

"That's okay," he said. "I can."

Her sense of pride had her telling him, "I can't ask you to do that."

He wasn't about to be dissuaded from this. "You're not asking. I'm volunteering."

She wanted to stand on her own two feet, even if those feet tended to be rather wobbly at the moment. "But—"

Jamie was happily kicking his feet in the sink, sending water over the side.

"And right now, you have a dripping son to take care of," Connor pointed out, shutting down her protest. "They get really pruney if they stay in the water too long."

Laughing at the image, Amy raised the little boy out of the sink. "Can't have that," she told Connor.

"See?" he asked, wrapping a towel around the wet baby. "We're in agreement—again."

Yes, Amy thought, they certainly were. More than Connor could possibly know.

## Chapter Seven

Rita wiped her hands on the apron that she wore almost perpetually around her waist and looked up at the two people who had walked into what she considered to be *her* kitchen. It was a little more than an hour after breakfast and she was in between routines when Connor approached her with a question.

"Of course you can leave the baby with me," Rita said, frowning at Connor. "Why would you think that you even have to ask me such a question?"

"Because I don't want to impose," Amy said, speaking up and answering the housekeeper's question before Connor could.

"There is that word again," Rita noted, shaking her head reprovingly. "*Impose.* Little ones do not impose," Rita informed the two adults standing before her. "*Adults* impose. Little ones are just there to bring joy into our lives."

"But an adult is asking you to watch him," Connor pointed out tactfully. There was no way he or any of his siblings wanted to run the risk of taking anything for granted when it came to the housekeeper. She was far too important to them and no one wanted to ruffle the woman's feathers.

Narrowing her eyes, Rita gave him an exasperated look.

"The *adult* would only be imposing if he was asking me to watch *him*," Rita informed him. "Now go, do whatever it is that you have to do. The baby and I will be waiting for you when you get back—and he will be changed and fed," the housekeeper added in case there were any lingering doubts about the baby's welfare.

Amy appreciated having Rita take care of Jamie until they got back, but at the same time, she knew that the woman's job description did not include watching over and taking care of a baby.

"But I don't want him interfering in your day," Amy said, still feeling somewhat uncomfortable about asking the woman to watch Jamie.

Rita's hands were on her hips, a sure sign that she was struggling to curtail her temper.

"Standing here and arguing with you is interfering with my day," the housekeeper informed them. "*Not* taking care of the little one. Now go. Shoo!" Rita ordered, waving them both on their way.

"You heard the lady," Connor said, taking hold of Amy's arm and ushering her toward the front door. "She wants us gone."

"I still don't feel right about this," Amy protested. "We could take Jamie with us," she said as Connor all but hurried her into her jacket. Once she had it on, he handed her her purse, which was hanging on a hook close to the front door.

"This'll go a lot faster if you don't have to worry about Jamie every other minute," he said, ushering her out of the house. "And if you feel bad about not bringing him into town, there'll be plenty of opportunities, I promise. For one thing—" he opened the passenger door for her and waited for Amy to get into his truck "—Miss Joan isn't going to give me any peace until I bring you and Jamie into the diner to see her."

Buckling up in the cab of the truck, Amy paused to look out the side window toward the house. "Maybe I should—"

"No," Connor said firmly, vetoing whatever stalling tactic she might have come up with. "Next time. You've been back in Forever for over two weeks and you haven't left the ranch once. It's time you got out a little. We'll stop at the law firm to talk to Cash and then we'll swing around to the center of town. Miss Joan had her minions bring down the annual Christmas tree from the forest yesterday and I hear there're still some branches left on it that need decorating."

Talking about the town's Christmas tree brought back a flood of memories to Amy. She turned in her seat to look at him. "Does Miss Joan really still pick the crew that has to go to pick out the tree?"

Connor laughed as he started the truck. That was the tradition that went back as far as he could remember. "Does the sun set in the west?"

"Nice to know that some things don't change," Amy told him with a nostalgic smile.

"Lots of things haven't changed," he assured Amy, slanting a glance in her direction.

She was smiling more these days, Connor observed, and he found that very heartening. It meant that Amy was slowly coming around, becoming her old self. Once her divorce was finalized and she shed one hundred seventy-five pounds or so of unwanted weight, he knew that she would breathe a lot easier—and then he'd see where they went from there.

For now he wasn't about to get ahead of himself—no matter how much he really wanted to.

It FELT AS if it took no time at all to reach Forever. All she did was blink and it seemed like they were there.

Her hands, Amy discovered when she looked down at them, were clenched and felt icy despite the gloves she'd thought to put on. That, she assumed, had more to do with her nervous state of mind than it did with any temperature drop.

She held the folder with all the papers she'd already filled out against her chest—a shield against all the things that had initially caused her to contemplate filing for divorce in the first place.

"Tell me again why we're going to Cash instead of Olivia," she said to Connor. "Wouldn't a woman be more sympathetic to my, um, situation?" Amy asked.

"Possibly," Connor allowed, a smile curving the corners of his mouth as he stated his reasoning. "But Cash is Miss Joan's stepgrandson and she is not about to allow him to leave any possible loopholes open that your former husband, that scum of the earth, might be able to use to keep you from getting that divorce."

She hadn't realized that Connor disliked Clay this

much. "Aren't you being a little hard on him?" Amy asked him.

Connor laughed drily. "I was just thinking that I was being way too easy and charitable on him." He spared her a glance. If he looked at her any longer, she'd see just how much he wanted to protect her, to take care of her. "Face it, Clay isn't in his right mind, Amy."

"What makes you say that?" she asked. Had Connor somehow heard something about Clay that she was unaware of?

"Easy," Connor answered her. "Because Clay cheated on you. No one in his right mind grabs hamburger just because it's there when he has filet mignon waiting for him at home."

She laughed at the image, as well as being referred to as filet mignon, as she stepped out of his truck. "You're just prejudiced," she told him, shrugging off Connor's flattery.

"I also have twenty-twenty vision," he said. "You're a beautiful woman, Amy. You don't need that poor excuse for a man hanging around, making you feel bad about yourself, undermining your self-esteem. The sooner you're legally rid of him, the better off you'll be."

She took a deep breath before responding. He was essentially preaching to the choir. "You're right, Connor."

"Of course I'm right." He opened the front door for her. "When it comes to this," he added, not wanting her to think he had some sort of inflated ego. That was Patton's territory. "Now let's go in."

The smile she offered him was definitely a nervous one and appeared to be a little frozen in place, but she managed to place one foot in front of the other and walked into the law firm of Santiago & Taylor.

The first person she saw was Cassidy, who was behind the reception desk. Cassidy's smile was warm and welcoming, and she found it comforting.

Cassidy rose to her feet. "About time you got around to coming here," she told Amy.

Amy looked over her shoulder at Connor, a silent question in her eyes.

"I never said a word to her. If I know Cassidy, she just put two and two together once I called to make the appointment for you."

"Oh." Amy nodded, accepting his explanation. She should have known better than to think Connor would have said anything that could be even remotely construed as gossip.

"Cash is waiting to see you," Cassidy told her. Coming around to the front of her desk, she said in her most official voice, "Right this way, please," and led them to Cash Taylor's office.

The latter faced Olivia's office. Both were of equal size even though Olivia had opened the law firm first. Cash hadn't officially transferred to Forever until he'd married Alma Rodriguez, the sheriff's former deputy.

Cash rose from his desk and crossed over to the couple, shaking Amy's hand first, then Connor's.

"Sit, please," he urged, gesturing to the two chairs that were facing his across the desk. "Make yourselves comfortable." He gave them a minute to do that before observing, "You didn't bring your baby."

"I thought it might go faster without him," Connor

told the other man. "You know how distracting babies can be."

Cash smiled, obviously thinking of his own brood at home. "You do have a point," Cash agreed. "But Miss Joan's going to be really disappointed."

"Oh, Miss Joan doesn't even know I'm in town," she said. "And even if she did, I can't believe that she'd even notice that I don't have Jamie with me."

Cash exchanged looks with Connor. "Oh, she'll notice, trust me," Cash assured her. "Miss Joan notices *everything* and she's very partial to babies."

"Next time," Amy said, realizing that maybe Connor and she had made a mistake leaving Jamie at home.

Cash nodded. "Just a little free advice," he confided. "If I were you, I'd make sure that 'next time' is very, very soon."

Amy inclined her head. "I'll remember that."

Laying the folder she'd brought on the desk in front of her and turning it around so that its contents were more readily accessible to Cash, she rested her hands in her lap and waited.

"Give me a moment," Cash requested. Taking out the papers she'd brought, he reviewed them quickly, paying special attention to the last page. "I see you signed the papers."

"Yes," Amy said, adding, "but Clay didn't."

Cash raised his eyes to hers. "Because…?"

"He didn't want to," she said bluntly. "He once told me that no matter how much I fought it, I was his property and I'd better get used to the idea." She looked at the lawyer, embarrassed that she had to confess something so degrading to him. "I guess that my question is, is there any way that I can divorce Clay if he refuses to ever sign the divorce papers? I just want to get him out of my life."

"Is there anything that can be done legally?" Connor asked the lawyer.

Amy was surprised by his serious tone of voice. Connor was usually so easygoing.

Cash nodded. "Absolutely. I can get you what's known as a contested divorce."

"I'm afraid I don't know what that is," Amy admitted.

She was trying not to allow herself to become too hopeful in case this all just wound up falling apart in the end.

"That's why you've come to me," Cash told her reassuringly. "When one spouse refuses to sign divorce papers, the proceedings can still move forward. A hearing is called to establish the reasons why Clay contests the divorce."

She couldn't see Clay willingly coming to court to have a judge hear him out and possibly rule against him. It was just something else his pride would prevent him from doing.

"What if Clay refuses to come to the hearing?" Amy asked. Following the law wasn't exactly Clay's style.

It was obvious that Cash was more than familiar with that sort of a situation. "Clay will be served with papers to make him aware of the hearing. If he still refuses to come to the hearing, then what you have is a divorce by default."

It was impossible to mistake the hope that sprang into Amy's eyes. "Does that mean—"

"Yes," Cash said. "It means you get the divorce and he gets to walk."

Amy felt like throwing her arms around the lawyer and hugging him hard with relief. She came very close to doing just that. "Really?"

Connor refrained from laughing at her eagerness.

"Really," Cash said.

"And this is legal?" Connor asked Miss Joan's step-grandson.

"Absolutely," he assured the couple as solemnly as he could manage.

Her smile could have lit up the entire office—and then some. She slid forward to the edge of her seat. "Then let's get started," she said eagerly.

"All right. I'm going to need a little more information from you." Cash glanced in Connor's direction. "Would you rather do this in private?" he asked Amy. "You have that right, you know."

"There's nothing I have to tell you that Connor can't hear," she told Cash. Smiling at Connor, she said, "If it wasn't for him, I wouldn't be here."

Cash nodded. "Fair enough. Then let's get started," he said, moving his keyboard closer so that it was more accessible.

"Well, that didn't take long," Connor commented as, less than an hour later, he and Amy left the small, squat building that housed the law firm.

Amy felt as if she was walking about five inches off the ground.

"Do you think Cash can really do what he said he could?" she asked Connor. She sounded a little breathless as she allowed herself to entertain the hope that she would finally be rid of Clay Patton in the very near future.

"I know there are some lawyers that will tell you anything you want to hear so they get you to sign on the dotted line just to get their hands on your money. But I also know," he went on quickly, "that Cash isn't one of those lawyers. And even if he were even mildly tempted to get you to sign on for some ulterior motive, Miss Joan is your temporary guardian angel and he is not about to go up against Miss Joan. No one in his or her right mind would knowingly consider doing that."

Amy bit her lower lip, thinking over what he'd just said. "I hope you're right."

He knew he was, but he didn't want to oversell it. Amy just needed to trust that things would work out for her.

"Speaking of Miss Joan," Connor said, steering her not toward his truck but toward the center of town, "there's only a limited amount of time for you to add a decoration to this year's annual Christmas tree."

But Amy dug in and held back. "I don't want to take that privilege away from someone from town."

"News flash, honey," the gravelly, whiskey-sounding voice coming from behind her said. "You *are* someone from town."

Startled, Amy swung around and found herself face-to-face with Miss Joan. Her heart felt as if it flipped over. Twice.

"Miss Joan, I didn't know you were behind me," she cried.

"Obviously," Miss Joan cracked. "Otherwise you wouldn't have been thinking of sneaking away from here like this."

"I wasn't sneaking," Amy assured the older woman. "I was just—"

"Sneaking," Miss Joan repeated. She pursed her thin lips as she looked around on both sides of Amy. "And where's that baby of yours?"

"Home—Connor's home," Amy quickly corrected herself. "He's sleeping."

"Uh-huh," Miss Joan murmured, still looking at Amy intently, as if the woman knew that it was just a matter of time before she would crack. "Well, since you are here and since there's only a limited amount of spaces left on the tree, go get yourself a decoration and hang it up. As a matter of fact, hang two, one for you and one for that baby of yours—*also* a citizen of Forever," Miss Joan said with conviction. She pointed toward the ground on the far side of the thirty-foot tree. "Decorations are over there. So's a ladder. Connor, I trust you can do the honors and hold that for her." Miss Joan turned on her heel and walked back to the diner, a queen returning to her castle.

## Chapter Eight

Amy laughed quietly to herself. "Five years and that woman hasn't changed a bit," she marveled as she watched Miss Joan return to the diner. Turning toward Connor, she asked, "How did she even know that I was out here by the tree? Or even in town, for that matter?"

"Like you said, Miss Joan hasn't changed a bit," Connor told her. "She's always had this innate ability to 'know' things. Either that, or the woman has radar," he said with a laugh. "Of course, there's a third choice. Cash could have called her and said that you'd been in to see him."

"What about lawyer-client confidentiality?" Amy asked.

"He didn't have to say *why* you came to see him, just that you did," Connor pointed out. "Actually, my money's on that woman just 'intuiting' your presence. C'mon," he urged, changing the subject. "Let's get you that decoration to hang up. I mean two decorations."

Amy appreciated that he was including Jamie, but that was overkill.

"Jamie's just a baby," she said, dismissing the need to hang up an extra decoration.

"That's why Miss Joan told you to hang up the decoration for him. Next year, if that boy's anything like the rest of the kids in town, Jamie'll probably want to hang up his own," Connor said.

Taking her elbow, he led Amy over to the remaining boxes of decorations that still had ornaments in them waiting to be hung up.

"We might not be here next year," Amy said quietly before she could think better of it.

Her words caught Connor off guard. He hadn't even *thought* about Amy wanting to stay anywhere else than in Forever. He stopped walking and looked at her quizzically.

"Why?" he asked. "Where will you be?"

She hadn't said it to upset him. She'd only been thinking out loud.

At one point, she would have said she was going to be with Clay for the rest of her life. But things hadn't gone according to plans—or dreams. So why should she think that anything else would.

But she didn't want to get into all that, so she just shrugged and said, "I don't know."

He could hear the note of indecision resonating in her voice. He'd backed off when he came to other questions— but not this time. "Don't you want to be here?"

"Yes, but I can't stay with you indefinitely," she said. The last thing she wanted to be was a burden to Connor.

"Let's just take this one step at a time, Amy. First we'll get you free of that poor excuse of a husband of yours," he said, tempering his reference to the man whose mere name made his blood boil, "and then we'll work on your living accommodations. Okay?" He gave her an encouraging smile.

He was trying so hard to help her and he was obviously solidly on her side. She felt her eyes misting. She'd been such a misguided idiot five years ago. How could she have not seen that he was the far better man?

"Okay," she answered.

"Time to pick out a decoration," he prodded, squatting down over the remaining open boxes.

There were still a great many to choose from, considering how many decorations were on the tree already. He looked over several ornaments before he finally picked up a large, shimmering snowflake dusted with silver sparkles applied to both sides.

"How about this one?" Connor asked, holding the snowflake aloft.

Amy smiled wistfully as she looked over the ornament. "That looks like something I would have made as a kid," she told him.

He considered that the seal of approval. "Perfect," he concluded, thrusting the snowflake into her hand. "Get in touch with the inner kid in you."

Amy's eyes crinkled. "Inner kid it is," she said, taking possession of the shimmering, patterned snowflake. "Now I just have to find a place to hang it," she said, slowly circling the giant tree. "Looks like all the lower branches are spoken for."

"That's why Miss Joan suggested you use the ladder," he reminded her. "I see a spot right up there." He pointed to a barren area just a foot above her head and to the left. He pulled the ladder over, setting it up as close against the tree as he could. "Don't worry," he said. "I'll hold the ladder steady for you. I won't let you fall."

"I wasn't afraid of falling," she told him with a toss of her head.

A fond smile curved his mouth. "As I remember, you weren't afraid of anything back in the day."

A wave of nostalgia brought a sad look in her eyes. More than anything, Amy wished she was still like that. "Yes, well, things change."

She sounded like she was talking more to herself than to him, Connor thought. Most likely she was thinking about something that Clay had done.

Wanting to keep the moment light for her, he asked, "Are you saying that you're afraid to climb up this ladder with me holding it for you?"

Amy appreciated what he was trying to do. It wasn't lost on her, but for the sake of playing along, she pretended to give him an impatient look. "Just hold the ladder."

"Yes, ma'am," he replied obediently, doing his best not to grin.

Connor stood to the side of the ladder, holding it so she could go up the first few rungs. Once she'd gone up three rungs, he moved to the center of the ladder, holding on to it on both sides as Amy climbed farther up.

The backs of her heels were level with his face when she finally reached her goal.

Maybe it was her imagination, but the ladder felt as if it wobbled slightly. "Don't let go yet," she warned.

Connor tightened his hands on both sides of the ladder. "I wouldn't dream of it," he told her.

Looking up, he saw that she was standing on the rung on her toes as she reached up as far as she could in order to hang the snowflake in an empty space. She was a few inches shy.

Amy was definitely making him nervous.

"Amy, why don't you come down and I'll hang that for you?" he offered, then pointed out the obvious. "I am taller than you are."

Amy gritted her teeth. "I can do this," she insisted. "Just hold on to the ladder." So saying, she climbed up another rung.

He could feel the ladder moving against his chest as he braced the ladder with his upper torso. "What do you think you're doing?" he demanded.

"Getting closer to the open space," Amy answered without looking down at him.

She was taking unnecessary chances for a Christmas ornament. Amy had had a daredevil streak as a kid and it was obviously making a comeback, he thought, irritated. He'd encouraged her to hang up an ornament, but not if it meant getting hurt.

"Amy, get down from there. You're going to break your neck," he called up the ladder.

Balancing herself on the rung, with one hand on the top of the ladder, she stretched her other arm as far as it would go.

"Not if you do your job right and hold on to the ladder for me," she answered.

Despite his best efforts, Connor could feel the ladder

straining and swaying even though he was gripping it for all he was worth. He could feel his biceps straining to steady the ladder—and consequently her—in place. It felt as if every single fiber of his being was fighting to hold the ladder—and her—upright.

This was getting to be really hard work. "You planning on coming down anytime soon, or have you decided to set up housekeeping up there?" he asked, raising his voice so that it carried up the ladder.

Having hung up the snowflake, she now had both hands on the ladder and braced herself for the descent. "I'm done with my decoration, but I still need to hang up Jamie's," she told him.

"Tell you what," Connor suggested, never taking his eyes off her. "You come down and we'll see if we can find any openings on the other side of the tree that are a bit closer to the ground for Jamie's ornament."

That sounded good to her. "All right. Hold the ladder steady," she told him. "I'm coming down."

As if he hadn't been trying to do just that all along.

His forearms as well as his biceps were straining—and trembling. These were muscles he obviously didn't use all that often, he thought, because despite all the heavy work he did around the ranch, his muscles now felt as if they were on fire as he struggled to hold the ladder perfectly steady until Amy had climbed down to a safer level.

And when she finally did that, he found that he had another problem, because he was now staring at a part of her anatomy that he had no business staring at. Even though he upbraided himself, he didn't look away immediately. Not for thirty whole seconds. It took that long for him to get a grip.

Why was she just staying there? Connor wondered. Was something wrong?

"You forget how to climb down the rest of the way?" he asked her.

"Not if you back off and give me a little more room," she answered. "I can almost feel you breathing on the back of my legs."

Obviously the grip he had on himself wasn't as effective as he thought. He masked his error with a quip. "That's a powerful imagination you have there," he said, taking great pains to give her as much room as possible to climb all the way down while still securing the ladder in place for her.

When she was finally on level ground again, Amy turned around and all but butted up against Connor's body. This time, they were face-to-face with less than half an inch between them.

He could feel her heart accelerating. He wasn't meant to be this close to her, he thought ruefully. Being this close totally destroyed his perspective and filled his head with all sorts of thoughts he couldn't afford to act on— or even be feeling.

There was no more public place than standing smack in the middle of Forever, yet all Connor could think about was kissing her. The only thing that stopped him was the threat of having Miss Joan pop up at any given moment and he would rather not have any witnesses around when he finally kissed Amy for the very first time—especially not Miss Joan.

Even if the woman didn't say anything at all, Connor knew he could almost hear her thoughts on the subject—something to the effect that it was "about time." As much as he liked Miss Joan, that was something he could do very well without.

He was more grateful to the woman than anyone would ever know, but that didn't mean he would willingly become her source of entertainment, at least not if that entertainment involved kissing Amy.

Clearing her throat, she stepped back. "I still have to find a spot where I can hang up Jamie's ornament," she reminded him. Amy took a deep breath, willing herself to get a grip and for her heart to settle down to a normal beat. She felt herself growing warmer and warmer and prayed that Connor wouldn't somehow see that in her face.

"A tree decorator's job is never done." Connor pretended to sigh dramatically as he temporarily closed the ladder, ready to drag it over to anywhere Amy saw fit to place it.

"Shh, let me concentrate," she told him, scanning every section slowly as she looked for a suitable space that wasn't prohibitively high up. "How many more decorations does Miss Joan intend to have people hang up?" she asked.

"As many ornaments as there are left in the boxes," he answered. And from what he could see, looking into the half-full boxes, there were still quite a bit left. "I think Miss Joan is going to have to get a bigger ladder," he said to Amy.

Amy pointed to a slightly barren area on the far side

of the tree and approximately five feet higher than she estimated she could reach standing on the ladder Connor was holding.

"How about over there?" she asked Connor, pointing out the space.

One look had him repeating, "Like I said, a bigger ladder."

She scanned the immediate—and not so immediate—area to see what else was available.

"There has to be at least one other ladder. A bigger one. Otherwise, how else did these other decorations get onto the tree?" she asked, pointing to the ornaments that were already on the tree and at least eighteen feet off the ground.

Without hesitation, he quipped, "Trained carrier pigeons."

"Very funny." She frowned at Connor, her hands on her hips. "No, seriously."

"Problem?"

The question came from Cody, who had walked up behind them without either of them hearing. The deputy had been observing his older brother and Amy and their efforts to hang an ornament on the town's Christmas tree from the shelter of the sheriff's office across the street.

"Ah, good. Looks like the cavalry's arrived," Connor commented.

"Not quite," Cody answered. "But if by 'cavalry' you're referring to common sense, then maybe you *are* right. Are you trying to reach that branch up there?" He pointed to the area that Amy had been looking at.

"It's a distinct possibility." Since Cody had a good

view of the square from the sheriff's office, Connor asked, "Where's the ladder that was used to decorate the upper section of the tree?"

"Probably back at the hardware store would be my guess," Cody told his brother.

Connor thought that was rather odd, considering the fact that the tree was still unfinished. "And how do we get a hold of that ladder?" Connor asked.

"You ask nicely," Cody said and then laughed at his own comment. "Look who I'm talking to." He regarded Connor with amusement.

Connor pinned him with a look. "What's that supposed to mean?"

"I haven't heard you asking nicely in years," Cody answered. "You're more the grumpy, demanding type these days."

"Did you ever think that was because I had to raise you three? Not the easiest thing to do considering how stubborn and headstrong all of you were. Lion tamers have an easier time of it." Connor started to head for the hardware store.

"Aren't you going to wait?" Cody asked him.

Connor stopped and looked at his brother quizzically. "Wait for what?"

"For the violins to accompany your story?"

He didn't mind exchanging banter with his brother, but right now he had something more important to take care of. "Are you going to help me get that ladder out of the hardware store or not?" Connor asked.

Cody pretended to look at him in surprise. "I have a choice?"

"No," Connor said flatly.

"Then I guess I'll help," Cody said, resigned. "Besides, having an officer of the law backing you up might be helpful in getting Jake to give you the ladder," he said, referring to the manager of the hardware store.

"We need the ladder to decorate Miss Joan's tree. She's all the backup that I need. I can, however, use some of that muscle of yours to carry that ladder from the hardware store over to the tree since it's so damn big. Why didn't they just leave the ladder out once they brought it over?" Connor asked. "It's not like someone was going to make off with it. The ladder is a little large to hide on your person."

Cody shrugged. "It's the hardware store's ladder and Jake was lending it out. He didn't owe anyone an excuse about why he wanted it back in the store."

"But the tree clearly isn't finished," Amy said, joining in.

Connor noticed that Cody's manner softened just a touch as he spoke to her. "Man probably has his reasons. His father still owns that store, and holding on to the oversize ladder when it's not being used might have been his idea. Maybe Jake didn't want to get into an argument with the old man." Cody looked pointedly at Connor. "You know how family can be sometimes."

"Yeah," Connor answered, looking directly at his younger brother. "Boneheaded."

Cody smiled. "My thoughts exactly."

Amy smiled. This felt just like old times. Before things had gone so awry. "It's the Christmas season, boys," Amy reminded the two men.

"You know, I think she's right," Connor said to his brother. "I guess we'd better go get that ladder so we can hang up Jamie's ornament." With that, he led the way to the hardware store.

## Chapter Nine

By the time Connor and Cody carried the borrowed ladder from the hardware store over to the Christmas tree in the town square, more than a few people had gathered around the tree, ready to press the ladder into service and hang up more ornaments.

However, both brothers made sure that Amy was the first one to make her way up the extended ladder in order to hang up her son's very first ornament on the town's Christmas tree.

Despite the exhilarated feeling she experienced in doing this for Jamie, Amy felt somewhat self-conscious as she made her way down the ladder. She wasn't accustomed to having an audience watching her every move.

The second her foot touched the ground and she stepped aside, the next person with an ornament immediately made his way up the ladder. Decorating the town's Christmas tree was a tradition that everyone relished and looked forward to.

Moving away from the gathering crowd, Amy told Connor, "I'm ready to go back to the ranch now."

She'd almost said "home" instead of "ranch" but she

had managed to catch herself just in time. She had to remember that it *wasn't* her home no matter how comfortable and familiar the ranch house might feel. It was *Connor's* home and she and Jamie were just temporary guests there, nothing more. She needed to keep that in mind, Amy silently lectured herself.

"You mean without stopping off at the diner first for a cup of coffee and some of my French fries you used to scarf up as a kid? Is that any way to treat an old friend?"

This time, Amy didn't have to turn around to know that Miss Joan was standing behind her again. How *did* the woman manage to keep doing that? Those comfortable shoes of hers seemed to be completely soundless.

They could at least squeak once in a while, Amy thought as she turned around to face the woman. She forced a smile to her lips.

"I thought I'd come by when I had the baby with me," Amy explained, hoping that was enough to get her off the hook with Miss Joan.

She should have known better.

"No reason you can't come by then, too," Miss Joan said matter-of-factly. "There're no restrictions posted on my door that say you can only stop at the diner a limited number of times in a week. If there was, half the people in town would starve to death," she added drily. "Now, are you coming, or do I have to get one of the McCullough boys to carry you to the diner?"

"Well, since you asked so nicely—" Amy began, trying to get a smile out of the woman.

"I wasn't asking, girl," Miss Joan informed her, her eyebrows narrowing. "I was *telling*. About time you learned the difference." The older woman turned on her soundless crepe heel and then led the way back to her diner.

Amy glanced at Connor. The latter gestured toward the diner owner's retreating back. "You heard the lady," he said.

Amy's eyes shifted to Cody, looking for support. She wasn't sure what the woman had in store for her.

"What he said," Cody told her, not about to go up against both his brother *and* the venerable Miss Joan.

It wasn't that she didn't want to go into the woman's diner. It was that she didn't relish the idea of being in close proximity to so many of Forever's citizens. The Christmas tree in the town square was a different matter. The people there were more interested in getting a chance to decorate the tree than they were in her return and what had prompted it.

But the diner wasn't just where everyone gathered to eat. It was also the place where everyone gathered to talk, to exchange news and, very bluntly, to gossip. Forever being the size that it was, there wasn't usually all that much to gossip about.

Until now, she thought as she went up the few steps to the diner's front door.

Connor held it open for her, waiting for her to go in ahead of him.

Sensing her tension, he leaned forward just as she crossed the threshold and told Amy, "It'll be fine. Remember, these were all your friends when you lived in Forever."

Friends she hadn't been in contact with for five years,

Amy thought ruefully. At first it was because she was so busy, trying to get her new home with Clay started. And then it was because she was too embarrassed to let those friends know that she'd realized she'd made a foolish, horrible mistake running off with Clay Patton. Whatever the cowboy might have had in looks and charm, he lost when it came to integrity and decency.

But that wasn't something she could just come out and say right off the bat.

To be honest, there wasn't a single thing she could share with these people about her last five years without either lying or humiliating herself.

"I've got to be getting back," Cody said. "See you next Sunday." The last sentence was addressed to both her and his brother just before he made his way back to the sheriff's office.

One step past the diner's threshold, she found herself hesitating to continue going. That was when she felt Connor taking her arm.

"It'll be all right," he said softly but with even more conviction. Then he added an order: "Breathe."

She could do that much, Amy thought, but she doubted it was going to be all right no matter what Connor told her.

"Come sit at the counter," Miss Joan called out, beckoning them to the front of the diner and patting the space she had selected for Amy. "Right up here where I can take a good look at you," she instructed as if she hadn't already scrutinized every inch of Amy twice over.

The space Miss Joan indicated would keep her directly under the older woman's watchful eye.

It also would keep anyone from approaching her with any invasive, probing questions or any harsh criticism. No one would dare do that to a person who was so obviously tucked under Miss Joan's protective wing.

"You take a drop of coffee in your cream, if I remember," Miss Joan said for form's sake—there was no *if* about it. Miss Joan never forgot anything. She poured a cup and set it before Amy. "And I just had a fresh batch of fries made less than five minutes ago," she told her as she placed a large order of fries in between Amy and Connor.

Steam was wafting enticingly from the offering.

"Well?" Miss Joan said, her hands on her hips as she waited for Amy to make a move. "Dig in before they get cold."

Amy did as Miss Joan urged and found, as the first fry disappeared between her lips, that it was hard not to smile. Not just at the taste, but at the memories that seemed to simultaneously burst on her brain as flavor burst along her tongue.

"There's more where that came from," Miss Joan told her as she moved toward another customer at the far end of the counter. "I'll be back to refill your cups and your plate," she promised, nodding at Connor.

The woman's unspoken instruction to him was clear. He was not to let Amy move until she'd finished what was on her plate.

"You're smiling," he observed, looking at Amy.

"Self-defense," she answered. "I think if I didn't, she'd start shooting questions at me." She looked down at the plate and the fries, which were quickly disappearing. "Her fries were always my favorite thing to eat. Nobody else makes fries like she does," Amy said nostalgically. "I don't know what it is that she does to them, but they definitely taste different." Two more fries disappeared between her lips.

"I always thought it was Angel's doing," Connor said, referring to the short-order cook Miss Joan had taken in several years ago and kept on at the diner even after Angel had married Gabriel Rodriquez.

But Amy shook her head. "No, she made them," she told Connor. "I *saw* her making them. I came in to the diner one afternoon, almost in tears because I was afraid I was going to fail my math course, and if I did that, I wouldn't be able to graduate. Miss Joan made me tell her what was wrong and then she said she knew what would cheer me up. I remember just mumbling something at her, saying something like 'Yeah, sure,' because even miserable, I knew you didn't argue with Miss Joan.

"And then she went in the kitchen and I could see her slicing up these potatoes, dusting this seasoning on them and then putting everything into the deep fryer. Ten minutes later, she had me smiling." Her mouth curved now, as she remembered the occasion. "I went on to not just pass that test but I got an eighty-nine on it. Miss Joan claimed there was something special in the fries that opened up my mind so I could use it to its full potential. Her words, not mine."

Amy laughed at herself. "I believed her, so much so that every time I had to take a test, the day before the test, I'd come in and ask Miss Joan for a plate of her 'special' fries. I know there was nothing magical about them, it was all the power of suggestion, but they did taste wonderful and I always felt better after having a serving."

Looking down at the plate, she realized that she'd taken the last fry.

"You want this?" she asked almost sheepishly, holding it up to Connor.

But he shook his head. "It's all yours," Connor told her.

As if on cue, Miss Joan made her way over to them again. She eyed the empty plate with smug satisfaction. "Want me to whip up another order?" the diner owner asked Amy.

Amy shook her head emphatically. "No. I'm stuffed, really. Thank you, though."

Miss Joan snorted as she gave her a disparaging look. "You eat like a bird."

"Birds actually eat quite a bit," Amy said. "They have to. They use up all that energy, constantly flying around."

"Not like some people I know who use up all their energy making up excuses," Miss Joan countered, looking at her pointedly. "All right," she agreed with a sigh. "Then you'll take an order of fries to go."

It wasn't a suggestion. The next moment, Miss Joan reached beneath the counter and produced a sealed foam container. She placed it on the counter in front of Amy.

"You had it ready for me?" Amy asked, surprised. "How did you know?"

The woman's thin lips moved to form the semblance of a smile for exactly half a second.

"Don't you know, girl? I know everything," the woman told her with an intense sense of satisfaction. "Okay, you can go home." She leveled a sharp look at Amy. "But I want to see that baby of yours before another week is out."

"Was that an order or a warning?" Amy asked Connor after he had settled up with the cashier and they made their way out of the diner, down the diner's steps.

"Both" was his guess. His truck was parked close to the door. He'd moved it once it was clear they were eating at the diner. Connor opened the passenger door for her. "I'm going to drop you off at the ranch," he told her.

He made it sound as if he wasn't coming in with her. "Aren't you going to stay at the ranch?" she asked.

"Sure," he said. "But first I've got an errand to run."

As far as she knew, errands brought people back into Forever. "You mean you're coming back to town?" she asked him.

"No" was all Connor would tell her in response.

THE TRIP BACK to the ranch was a quiet one.

Connor was being mysterious about this "errand" of his, Amy thought, but she didn't feel she had the right to pry and ask questions. She was his guest, a guest who had practically pushed herself into his house. That gave her no right to ask questions or to interfere in his life, at least not any more than she felt she already had.

So she kept to herself the questions that were popping up in her head and multiplying like amorous rabbits hopped up on steroids.

The fact that she found herself suddenly wondering

if Connor was seeing someone he had been neglecting because of her was a notion she had to keep to herself.

But the thought of Connor driving off to see a girl-friend had her feeling agitated and tied her stomach up in knots.

Amy found herself wanting to sit down somewhere secluded with the second order of Miss Joan's special fries.

Or even a third.

*C'mon. Grow up*, Amy silently ordered as she forced herself to seek out Rita in an effort to distract herself—and to behave like a responsible mother.

"Did he give you any trouble?" she asked the woman as she walked into the kitchen. Jamie was nearby in the cradle, asleep.

"Far less trouble than the grown-ups in this house," Rita informed her. The woman stopped chopping carrots to take a closer look at her face. "Is everything all right, Miss Amy?" she asked.

"Everything's fine," Amy answered automatically and maybe a bit too quickly.

The last thing she felt like doing was elaborating on what was gnawing away at her. Besides, Rita's loyalty would be to Connor, not to her. She wouldn't be able to get any information out of the woman.

Rita regarded her skeptically, obviously not convinced that everything was fine.

"Where is Mr. Connor?" the housekeeper wanted to know.

Amy shrugged. "He said he had to run an errand," she said.

She should have known that wouldn't be enough for the housekeeper. "What kind of an errand?" Rita asked.

"He didn't say and I didn't ask." At least she didn't have to lie to the woman. The woman obviously could see through lies. "I'm going to go see if Jamie needs anything," she said by way of excusing herself from the woman.

Or trying to.

Rita raised her voice the second she turned away from the housekeeper. "I changed him ten minutes ago and he ate half an hour ago. He fell asleep in my arms, and as you can see, he is still sleeping, but you are free to stand over him and wait for him to wake up," Rita told her.

"I think I'll just go into my room for a few minutes," Amy said.

"Or you could stay here and help me with dinner."

Very quietly, Amy went to the cabinet and opened the cutlery drawer directly beneath it. Finding what she was looking for, she pulled out a long knife and took it to the counter.

Rita slid a second cutting board in her direction without even glancing up. Obligingly, Amy stood beside the housekeeper and began chopping carrots.

## Chapter Ten

Jamie slept through all the chopping, completely oblivious to the sound created by knives meeting wooden cutting boards. He continued sleeping as Rita, with Amy's help, finished preparing all the ingredients that she needed to make the beef stew that Connor favored.

Combining the ingredients, Rita put everything in an oversize pot and had it simmering on the back burner of the stove.

Rita had begun clearing the counter, putting things away into the pantry, while Amy had just sunk down in a chair at the table, when they suddenly heard a loud commotion coming from the living room.

As did Jamie.

The noise woke the baby up and he quickly made his displeasure known by immediately putting his newly rested lungs to work.

Amy was instantly on her feet and heading toward the cradle. Since she was closer, Rita got there ahead of her and picked Jamie up.

Patting the baby on his little back and murmuring

something in Spanish softly in his ear, the housekeeper turned to face her.

"I will take care of him. You go see why Mr. Connor is making all that noise."

"How do you know it's Connor?" Amy asked, already crossing the kitchen on her way toward the living room.

"Because if he was a thief, he would be quieter about breaking in," Rita answered without so much as a hint of a smile.

The first thing Amy saw when she reached the entrance to the living room was Connor with his arms wrapped around a tall, rope-bound evergreen. He was plainly struggling to drag the tree farther into the room without damaging anything in his path.

From her vantage point, it looked to her as if Connor was dancing with the tree and the tree looked as if it might be leading.

"Connor?" Amy asked uncertainly, coming closer to him and the tree. "What are you doing?"

If he turned around, Connor had a feeling that he would wind up pulling the muscles in his neck, so for now he gave his answer still looking at the tree.

"What does it look like I'm doing?" he said. "I'm trying to bring a Christmas tree into the house without losing all the needles before I can actually get to put the tree up."

Amy hurried over to grab the bottom of the tree. Lifting it off the floor, she helped Connor carry the tree the rest of the way into the room.

"You cut down a tree?" she asked him, surprised. He

hadn't said anything about putting up a Christmas tree in the ranch house.

"Well, trying to pull it out by its roots wasn't working out, so yes, I cut the tree down," Connor deadpanned, measuring out his words and trying not to pant.

"Why didn't you tell me this was the errand you were running?" she asked. "I would have gone with you to help."

He paused for a second to look over his shoulder and make sure they were heading in the right direction.

"Amy, in case you failed to notice, you're a hundred and three pounds and no match for a tree. I couldn't pick both you and the tree up at the same time."

Her end of the tree was getting heavy, but she was determined to hold it up, especially after what Connor had just said.

"I'm not the weakling you think I am," she informed him crisply, doing her best not to pant. "Where are we taking this, anyway?"

"Well, I was seriously thinking of taking the tree for a walk, but for now, let's just set the end down here," he told her. Backing up to the corner, he leaned the tree precariously against the wall as best he could. "I'm leaving the tree against this corner while I go get the Christmas tree stand out of the attic."

Amy got in front of him quickly, stopping him in his tracks.

"You're winded," she said. "Tell me where to find the tree stand and I'll go bring it down for you."

Connor shook his head. "It would take me longer to

give you the directions than it would to go fetch it my-self."

But Amy refused to budge as she looked at him im-patiently. "I'm not entirely clueless, Connor. I can fol-low directions."

"No, you're not clueless at all," he was quick to agree. And then he sighed and capitulated. "Okay, you win. The tree stand should be right in front of the boxes of Christmas decorations. There should be a broken cuckoo clock right next to it."

Amy nodded. "Okay, got it."

He caught her hand for a moment. "Are you sure you want to go crawling around in the attic?"

She flashed him a smile. "I'm sure."

"Don't forget to watch out for the spiders," he called after her.

She knew Connor was saying that just to get her to change her mind about climbing into the attic—or at least she hoped so.

"The spiders are going to have to watch out for *me*," she fired back over her shoulder as she continued walk-ing out of the room.

With a sigh, Connor settled back on the sofa and waited for her to come back. He had to admit, it felt good to rest.

It was taking too long, Connor thought.

He glanced at his watch. It shouldn't have taken Amy longer than ten minutes to climb into the attic, find the tree stand and climb back down again. It was going on almost twice that length of time and she hadn't come back downstairs yet.

"Damn," he muttered under his breath as he got up off the sofa. He should have put his foot down and told her he was going to get the tree stand.

What if she *had* gotten bit by some rare spider in the attic? Or possibly by a mouse or a rat? And now that he thought of it, there were all kinds of things haphazardly piled up in the attic. What if she'd tugged on the stand and caused a whole bunch of boxes to topple on her?

All sorts of scenarios went through his head by the time Connor got to the drop-down stairs that fed into the attic. Rather than call out her name, he saved his breath and just started climbing up.

If anything had happened to her, it was all on him. He had to learn how to say no to Amy.

Scanning the dimly lit area the moment he poked his head up inside the attic, he saw her. Amy was sitting cross-legged on the floor, her back partially to him, the Christmas stand sitting right next to her.

But it wasn't the stand that had her attention. It was the huge, dusty album in her hands. She was paging through the pictures in it.

Connor slowly exhaled, releasing the tidal wave of tension that had been building up within him. She wasn't hurt; she was just distracted. Climbing up the rest of the way into the attic, he approached her, doing his best not to startle her.

"What are you looking at?" he asked her.

Ordinarily, Amy would have jumped, surprised to hear someone talking to her when she thought she was completely alone. But for some reason, in this instance, the sound of Connor's voice felt appropriate, blending in with the photographs she was looking at.

"The past," Amy answered, then became a little more specific. "*Our* past. I'd forgotten how cute you looked in high school. Cute and serious." She beckoned him over to her so he could see what she was looking at. She held up the album so he could get a better view. "You looked so very determined, like you were ready to take on the world the second they handed you your diploma."

Connor sat down next to her, peering at the photographs. "I was," he said. And then he reflected on how losing his father had changed everything for him as well as for his brothers and sister. "And I did. Just not the way I thought I was going to," he confessed.

Instinctively she knew what he was referring to. There was a time when she and Connor were pretty in sync with one another, sharing thoughts, ending each other's sentences. Why hadn't she seen that for what it was worth? If she had, then Clay wouldn't have dazzled and blinded her the way he had.

"That was pretty great of you," she told him quietly, "sticking around and becoming your brothers' and sister's guardian."

He shrugged off her compliment. "I didn't do anything any one of them wouldn't have done if the tables were turned," he said, sincerely believing that. "You can bring that down if you want to look through it some more, but right now, we'd better get downstairs with the tree stand unless you want to see one annoyed little woman climbing up into the attic to give us a long lecture for taking too long up here."

"Rita's liable to hurt herself, climbing up here," Amy said, concerned as she pictured the housekeeper doing that.

He laughed, getting to his feet and then extending his hand to Amy. "I wouldn't doubt that she's probably more agile than we are."

"Now that you mention it, I'd rather not put that to the test," Amy admitted.

Taking the stand, she slowly made her way down out of the attic. Connor followed, pausing to raise the stairs back up into the ceiling before he went all the way back down to the living room.

The baby was back in his cradle and Rita was finishing up in the kitchen. She gave Connor an unfathomable look as he passed her.

"What?" he asked.

"Nothing," she replied in a disinterested voice. "It was just that you were up in the attic for so long, I thought you forgot all about the tree that you dragged into the house *and* about dinner," she added with emphasis, "and decided to *live* in the attic."

"And miss out on all your good cooking?" Connor asked, his hand on his chest as if to keep his heart from leaping out. "Never happen. Amy just found an old album and we were looking at our old school pictures."

"Uh-huh," the housekeeper answered.

He was *not* about to ask her what she meant by that. Some things he was just better off not knowing.

Walking into the living room, he put down the tree stand next to the tree he'd brought in.

"How do you want to do this?" Amy asked, looking at the tree. She was ready and eager to get started.

But there was a lot of work involved with putting up their own tree and decorating it. Having Amy there had made him temporarily forget all that and only think about sharing the celebration with her.

"Tomorrow," he answered.

She looked at him, confused. "I don't understand. Why go through all this trouble if you're just going to leave the tree leaning against the wall like this?" she asked.

"Seeing the tree in the town square made me want to hurry up and get one for our Christmas—the ranch's Christmas," he corrected, not wanting her to think he was pressuring her to think of this in any sort of personal terms. "But now that I've got this here, I figure it'll be a lot easier if I get Cole to help me lower the tree into the stand. If Cole and I both hold on to it, we can keep it straight and you can tighten the screws in the stand until the tree is secured."

She nodded. "Sounds good."

And what sounded *really* good to her was that Connor was including her in this. It felt wonderful to be part of getting the house ready for the holidays. It gave her a warm feeling.

She'd done her best the last five years to infuse the spirit of Christmas into the house that she and Clay rented, but very early on, it had gotten to the point where Clay was far more interested in going out with his friends, drinking and gambling, than he was in being home with her, celebrating Christmas or anything else.

"It's almost dinnertime," Connor told Amy. "I'd better go get cleaned up before Rita starts giving me dirty looks."

He began to walk by Amy when he saw a tear sliding down her cheek. Connor stopped.

"Amy?"

She turned her head away, trying to hide her face, afraid he'd spotted her tears. She pressed her lips together, doing her best to sound as if there was nothing wrong.

"What?"

Taking hold of her shoulder to keep her from trying to walk away, Connor used his other hand to turn her head toward him. His gut tightened when he saw the tears. Was this about Clay? Was she thinking about him and missing him?

"Amy, are you crying?" he asked her gently.

"I've got allergies." She sniffed.

"Oh." Because he didn't want to embarrass her, he pretended to believe her, hoping that eventually she would open up to him. "Do you take anything for that?"

"No. Most of the time they go away on their own." She cleared her throat so that she wouldn't sound as if she was choking up—or worse, start crying uncontrollably.

Connor took out his handkerchief and handed it to her.

"They can be a real bear, allergies," he said sympathetically. "Well, like I said, I'm going to go and get cleaned up. Maybe by the time I get back, your allergies will stop bothering you."

Amy took in a long breath and then let it out again. "Maybe."

AMY'S EYES WERE still a little red when she sat down at the table several minutes later, but there was no more evidence of tears.

After bringing the large tureen filled with stew to the table, Rita set it down, resting the ladle beside it. Automatically wiping her hands against her apron, she looked at the two occupants at the table and zeroed in on Amy.

Amy braced herself for an interrogation, or at the very least, a shower of endless questions. The housekeeper didn't seem to make a secret of the fact that she felt it was her right to know everything that was going on with the people who lived in the house.

Instead, Rita merely nodded her head as if in response to some internal comment she'd made to herself. And then out loud she said, "The attic can be a very dusty place. Sometimes too dusty." She looked from Amy to Connor, her expression completely unreadable. "Memories create dust." And then the woman abruptly changed the subject.

"The stew is very hot. Be careful not to burn your mouths eating it. If you do, that will not go away in a day or two. It will make everything else—like brushing your teeth—very difficult for you." She said it in all seriousness, as if she was imparting one of the lessons of life.

Amy exchanged a glance with Connor. They both knew the housekeeper wasn't talking about something as mundane as brushing teeth. Amy found herself struggling not to laugh.

"Good advice, Rita. We'll wait for the stew to cool off. That way we won't burn our tongues or mouths,"

Connor told the woman with such a straight face, for a second, Amy thought he was being serious.

Only the twinkle in his eye gave him away.

## Chapter Eleven

"Well, this is new," Cole commented as he let himself into the house and walked into the living room early the next morning. Connor was already in the room.

Cole moved in closer to inspect the tree that was still propped up in the corner where it had been left the day before. Because it had yet to be placed into the tree stand, the ropes remained securely tied around the tree.

Cole glanced over toward his brother. "You holding the tree for ransom or something?"

"I left the ropes on until I could get some help putting the tree up," Connor answered. "It's too unwieldy otherwise."

"Isn't this a little early for you?" Cole asked, curious. "You usually don't get a tree until right before Christmas. Last year you said you were thinking of not even bothering with a tree this time around."

Connor remembered. He had said that because Cody and Cassidy had moved out into their own homes with their own families, and he'd had a feeling that Cole wasn't going to be far behind. To his way of thinking, a single man didn't need to have a huge Christmas tree.

Decorated and all lit up, it only served to remind him of all the things that he *didn't* have.

"Changed my mind," Connor told his brother. "Besides, if I'm going to go through all this trouble of lugging in and decorating a tree, I might as well do it sooner and have it around longer."

Cole nodded his head. "So you're planning on hanging on to it until it turns into kindling and poses a fire hazard. Smart," he said sarcastically.

Connor gave his brother an annoyed look.

"Not that long," Connor retorted. "Now, are you going to help me get it into the tree stand, or are you just going to stand around and yap all day?"

"You mean I've got a choice?" Cole asked as if that was a serious consideration.

Connor's eyes narrowed. He just wanted to get the tree up so he could get to work outdoors. Yesterday had turned out to be a lost day, not that he minded in the least how he'd wound up spending it, but the horses couldn't be neglected for too long.

"Just get your butt over there and help me center this tree over the stand," he told his brother.

Amy had walked in on the tail end of the exchange. She smiled a greeting at Cole.

"See how he treats me?" Cole pretended to complain to her.

"Don't pay any attention to him, Amy," Connor countered. "Just get ready to tighten the screws against the tree trunk when I tell you."

"You're finally putting the tree up?" she asked, excited over the prospect of decorating the tree.

It was really a rhetorical question. Amy quickly grabbed the stand and pulled it over, ready to help in any way she could.

Getting down on her knees between the two brothers, she quickly positioned the stand so that the moment they picked the tree up, the stand would be directly underneath it.

"Whenever you're ready," she said.

As Connor and Cole carefully picked up and then lowered the tree, Amy made sure the stump was inside the stand. When it was, she began to work the screws, tightening first one, then the other, then the third, turning each equally so the tree would wind up going in straight.

"The screws are all as tight as they can go," Amy announced from beneath the tree.

"Get out from under there," Connor told her, "and then we'll let go of the tree and see if it's actually straight."

"And stable," Cole added. He still had a good hold on the tree and didn't look as if he was inclined to let the tree go. "Don't forget stable."

"Don't be so skittish," Connor said, recalling one incident with the tree that went less than smoothly. "The tree only fell on you once."

"Once was enough," Cole assured him.

"The tree fell on you?" Amy cried, still on the floor on her stomach as she made adjustments to the stand.

"Only because Cassidy jostled it," Connor said. "We hadn't finished tightening the stand on the trunk—it was a case of too many cooks spoiling the stew."

"Stew wasn't nearly as heavy as that tree was," Cole recalled.

"Stop sounding like an old lady," Connor admonished.

Crouching slightly, he gave Amy his hand and helped her to her feet. Once she was up, they all took a step back away from the tree.

"What do you think?" he deliberately asked her, not Cole, as he regarded the tree critically.

Amy slowly circled the still-bound Christmas tree. "Looks straight to me," she finally pronounced. "Of course, it'll look a lot better once you cut the ropes and the branches fill out the silhouette a little more."

Connor glanced at his brother. "Cole?"

"Yeah, looks pretty straight to me," he agreed.

"Okay," Connor said, "only one thing left to do." He went to get something to cut with out of the kitchen.

Amy and Cole heard Rita issue a protest. "Not my carving knife!"

When Connor walked back into the living room, he shook his head. "I swear that woman gets more possessive every day. She's going to think she owns everything in the house in another couple of years."

Amy suppressed a grin. "Is that hers?" she asked, nodding at the knife that Connor had in his hand.

"No," he told her, cutting away the ropes. "It's a different one."

He made short work of the ropes he'd initially tied around the tree he'd cut down yesterday and they fell to the floor around the tree in an uneven circle. Setting the knife aside, Connor shook out various sections of the tree, coaxing the branches to fill out.

"So I take it we're spending the rest of the day decorating your tree?" Cole asked once the branches had all responded and the Christmas tree looked full and healthy.

"No," Connor answered as Amy gathered up the ropes from the floor. "The horses need to be fed, watered and groomed, and there's some more work to be done on that fence we were working on. We lost a full day yesterday and it has to be made up somehow."

"What about the tree?" Amy asked him, putting the pieces of rope on the coffee table.

"We can decorate the Christmas tree slowly. The important thing is that we got it up," he told her. "And don't forget, Miss Joan expects to see you and the baby, so we need to go into town."

"Today?" Cole asked, surprised.

"No, not today. I don't have the time," Connor pointed out. "But it has to be soon. You know how Miss Joan is. She doesn't like being left out of anything."

"And she shouldn't be," Cole agreed. "If it wasn't for her, we would have all gone hungry and done without more than a few times."

Rather than bristle at the reminder the way Clay might have, Amy thought, Connor wholeheartedly agreed.

"Preaching to the choir, boy. Preaching to the choir," he told his brother.

Cole cocked his head in the direction of the back bedroom. "Speaking of choir, sounds to me like an angel just woke up. An angry angel," Cole qualified with amusement as he looked in Amy's direction.

Amy nodded. She was glad that Jamie had slept for as long as he had. "I'll go see what he wants," she said, heading to the guest bedroom. She'd brought the baby down in the wee hours of the morning and put him into the cradle, wanting to keep him close by as she helped with the tree.

But Connor caught her hand, keeping her in place. "I'll go," he said. "Might as well see him while I'm still here."

Bemused, Cole looked at his brother, then at Amy, giving her a look of confusion. Amy smiled.

"I think your brother's a baby whisperer," she told him. "No matter how much Jamie's fussing, all Connor has to do is pick him up and start talking to him and just like that, Jamie's all smiles."

Cole laughed as he nodded knowingly. "Well, Connor's had four other babies to train on. And he does seem to have a knack for this sort of thing," Cole agreed. "I saw it right from the start, when Cody brought Devon's baby to the house. Personally, I think that babies think Connor's another baby, just like them—except that he's a little large for his age."

"I heard that," Connor said, coming back into the room.

"Well, at least your hearing's still good, so you can't be getting that old," Cole teased.

Connor gave him a dismissive look. "I'll show you old. Try and keep up with me out there today," he challenged.

"Ha!" Cole laughed. "No problem."

"Amy, I believe this is yours," Connor said, transferring the baby into her arms.

The moment he left the shelter of Connor's arms,

Jamie made a noise that sounded suspiciously like a protest.

"See," Amy said to Cole, "he's fussing already. I told you, there's something about Connor that just calms him right down."

"That's because Connor's boring," Cole said, darting out of the way before Connor could cuff him.

"Don't pay any attention to him," Connor said, addressing the baby. Looking up, he met Amy's eyes. "I'll keep my cell phone on me. Call if you need me. Otherwise, I'll see you tonight," Connor told her just before he left.

"Does she know what a big deal that is?" Cole asked as his brother closed the door behind him.

"What are you talking about?"

"You keeping your cell phone on you," Cole said as they got into Connor's truck and headed for the main stable. "You hate that thing."

"This is the twenty-first century. Concessions have to be made," Connor answered without looking at his brother.

"Yeah, right. Concessions," Cole echoed, then laughed as if he knew Connor was just making excuses.

Connor decided it was better not to respond.

"OKAY, LITTLE MAN," Amy said to the baby in her arms as she turned away from the door, "time to feed you breakfast—and then we'll figure out what we're going to do with the rest of your day. Sound good?"

Jamie made some sort of a noise that was half a squeal, half a gurgle.

Amy smiled. She was feeling a great deal more relaxed these days than she had during the first six months of Jamie's life. Then she was always worried that the baby would cry, causing Clay to yell at her and Jamie. The atmosphere had gotten incredibly tense.

Being here was good for Jamie, she thought. And for her. And that, she knew, was all Connor's doing, bless him.

After feeding the baby and herself, Amy spent some time playing with the little boy, but it wasn't all that long before he became drowsy and wound up napping again. She put him back into the cradle.

At loose ends, Amy decided to bring down at least some of the decorations out of the attic. She didn't think Connor would mind her doing that. Besides, it would be saving him some extra work, she told herself. Most men didn't like to have to bring boxes down out of the attic, or be stuck taking decorations out of those boxes, for that matter.

Clay never made any attempt to help with the decorations. Not even in the very beginning. What she did remember him doing was complaining that the decorations cost too much money even though, most of the time, she was the only one who was working and she paid for the decorations.

"I'm going to get some of the ornaments out of the attic," she told Rita in case the woman suddenly needed to talk to her.

Rita nodded, as if she'd expected her to do that all along.

"Unless you need me for something," Amy qualified, thinking that the housekeeper might appreciate the help.

Rita gave her one of her unfathomable looks. "Why would I need you for something?" she asked.

"Just in case," Amy said.

Rita waved her off. "Go. Your son's sleeping. Do whatever you want to do."

Amy didn't have to be told twice.

She shouldn't have left Forever so quickly, Amy lamented ruefully as she made her way up into the attic.

Or at all, she amended. But her dad had died and her mother had remarried. Her mother's new husband had wanted to move to California, the sooner the better. With no family in Forever, she felt there wasn't really anything there for her anymore.

It was while she was finding her way around in this pit of loneliness that Clay swept into her life like a twister, snatching away her breath and apparently all of her common sense, she thought now as she selected a number of boxes to bring downstairs.

Making her way down the ladder carefully, Amy continued reviewing her past. She wished she had thought things out more carefully. Wished she had seen Connor as more than just a friend back then.

Because he was *so* much more. She felt her pulse begin to rush the way it did every time she started to think about him.

*You're leaning on him too much. Depending on him too much*, she warned herself fiercely. If she wasn't careful, she'd wind up scaring him away or making him regret taking her in. Then where would she be?

She was seeing him in a romantic light and he was probably seeing her just as a friend, the way he always had. Connor had always been a very good friend to her, and if she wasn't careful, she was going to wind up losing that.

*Stop it. You've got things to do, not moon around about Connor. You can't pay him back for his kindness by acting like some lovesick, desperate female.*

*Get busy,* she ordered herself.

Amy divided the rest of her morning between looking in on Jamie—tending to him whenever he needed something—and bringing down the rest of the Christmas decorations.

Initially, she'd meant to bring down only a box or two. Or maybe three.

She wound up bringing them all down. And then, after lunch, having nothing to occupy herself with after she helped clear the table—Rita insisted she didn't need any help with preparing dinner—Amy slowly took all the ornaments *out* of their boxes, lining them up on the floor near the tree like colorful little soldiers waiting to be pressed into service.

Unable to resist, once she had all the decorations unpacked and ready, she hung a few of the ornaments up, placing a few here and there. She did it to give the tree a little life and make it look more like a Christmas tree than a tree that had been brought into the house to be sheltered from whatever storms might eventually be out there.

Unable to find a ladder, Amy dragged a chair over to the tree so she could hang some of the ornaments up higher. Climbing onto the chair, she started to hum Christmas carols.

That was how Connor found her. Humming Christmas carols to herself, standing on a chair and hanging an ornament up on one of the upper branches.

Watching, he felt something warm tug at his heart at the same time that something in his gut tightened. Hard.

If he could have, he would have stood there like that all evening, just watching Amy hang up ornaments. But he knew she was bound to turn around and see him. He didn't want her to feel self-conscious or uncomfortable. Most people didn't like being caught off guard, and humming while decorating a Christmas tree easily fell under that category.

"I see that you took down all the ornaments out of the attic," he said, coming forward.

She turned around and he saw her cheeks redden. It was a definite improvement over the tearstains he'd seen on them yesterday.

A flash of guilt crossed her face, as well.

"I'm sorry," she apologized. "I didn't think you'd mind."

Taking her hand, he helped her down from the chair. "No need to apologize," he told her. "I just didn't want you to do all that work by yourself."

"Well, it wasn't like I had to clear my schedule," she said with a laugh. "Jamie was pretty well behaved today after his session with you, and Rita absolutely didn't need my help with *anything*. She made a point of telling me that more than once. So I thought, since you brought this beautiful tree into the house, the least I could do was get down all the Christmas decorations from the attic for you. Once I had them down, I would have left them there, but I still had nothing to do, so I started slowly taking them out of the boxes."

"You didn't have any trouble carrying all those boxes down from the attic?" Connor asked skeptically.

"I juggled them," Amy deadpanned. Then, unable to carry it off, she laughed. "No, I just kept going up and down until I brought down all the boxes." She looked at the tree. "I was going to wait until you got home before I hung up anything, but I thought you wouldn't mind if I did one or two."

"No, I don't mind," he told her. "I'm just glad you left the rest of the ornaments for us to hang up together."

She looked at him in surprise. "You like decorating the Christmas tree?"

"Actually, it's one of my very favorite things," Connor admitted. "It reminds me of when my mother was alive. She and Dad used to each take a side of the tree and pretend to compete to see who 'did the better job' decorating. Dad always said he let Mom win because it made her so happy." His smile widened as he recalled the memory. "Mom always said she won because she was so good at it."

Amy felt wistful. She found herself wishing she had memories like that to look back on. "Sounds like they both won."

"Well, I don't know about them, but I know that I sure did. So did Cole and Cody. Those were some of the happiest days of our lives."

"Are you two going to stand there and talk all evening, or are you going to come into the dining room and have dinner?" Rita asked. She was standing in the doorway, looking at them reprovingly.

"We'll come and have dinner, of course," Connor told the combative housekeeper. Taking Amy by the arm, he said, "Let's go, Amy. The tree can wait."

*Yes*, she thought. *It certainly can.*

It gave her something to look forward to.

## Chapter Twelve

*Practice makes perfect*, Amy thought with a smile as she tiptoed out of the baby's bedroom where she'd put him to bed for the night.

She had gotten very good at getting Jamie fed, changed and ready for bed. However, it did take her a bit longer this evening before she managed to get him to go to sleep. The minute his bright blue eyes closed and his breathing had taken on the easy, steady cadence, Amy headed straight downstairs for the living room and the Christmas tree.

Connor was waiting for her.

He'd opted not to do any more decorating until Amy could come down to join him. To his way of thinking, this decorating for Christmas was more for her benefit than for his.

Watching her now, he couldn't help laughing. "I've never seen anyone pick up an ornament so fast before."

She flushed a little, embarrassed that perhaps she seemed just a little too eager. But the truth of it was that she *was* eager. All her suppressed feelings about the season finally had an avenue of escape.

"I thought you'd get started without me," she told Connor.

"What's the fun in that? The whole idea behind decorating a Christmas tree is having someone to do it with," he told her simply. He saw that his words had generated a sad smile on her lips in response. That hadn't been his intent. "What?"

Amy shrugged self-consciously. She shouldn't be dwelling on sad memories. This was a happy time. "All the Christmases I spent with Clay, he never once offered to help me decorate the tree. The first year, when I asked him to come with me to pick one out, he said he thought the whole thing was a waste of time and money. He told me that if I really wanted to have a Christmas tree, I had to get one of those small artificial trees so I wouldn't be constantly throwing out money, buying a new one every year." Reaching up, she hung a small silver bell on one of the higher branches. "It never quite felt like Christmas to me, decorating a little fake tree, but then, I suppose it was better than nothing," she said philosophically.

"Well, careful what you wish for," he said with an amused smile. "You're going to be decorating a ten-footer this time around."

"Not by myself," she said, looking at Connor, her meaning clear.

"No," he readily agreed. "Not by yourself." Stepping back, he took a long, thoughtful look at the tree. He *knew* he'd forgotten something. "As a matter of fact, maybe before you put another single decoration up, I should get the lights up first."

Taking a second look at the tree, Amy realized he was right. She'd been so eager to decorate the tree, she'd gotten ahead of herself. The lights definitely needed to go on first.

"Tell me what you want," she told Connor. "I'm ready and willing to help."

What he wanted, Connor thought, was to take that delicate face of hers between his hands, lower his mouth to it and kiss her. That had nothing to do with decorating a tree and everything to do with bringing the spirit of Christmas to life.

At least for him.

It would also, he thought ruefully, scare Amy right out of the ranch house and possibly out of the state, as well. So, focusing on the issue at hand, Connor answered, "You can try to keep the tail end of the string from tangling while I hang up these lights."

"That's all?" she asked, disappointed and feeling a little useless.

He pulled over the box that contained the strings of lights and opened it. He frowned as he looked down into the box and contemplated its contents: lots and lots of tangled-up Christmas lights.

"Believe me," Connor said, loosening the first string he found, "that's a lot. Tangled-up strings of Christmas lights definitely take the merry out of Christmas, at least for me."

"Then I'll do my very best to untangle them for you and keep them that way," Amy promised.

They got started.

She felt a little silly following him around in what

amounted to circles as Connor attached the lights to the uppermost branches and worked his way slowly down and around the tree.

It took well over an hour and involved five separate strings with a total of countless multicolored lights on each string, but in the end, he'd managed to cover the entire ten-foot tree with Christmas lights.

He plugged the end of the connected strings into a wall socket, and the tree came to brilliant life.

"It's beautiful," Amy murmured with a note of awe in her voice. She stepped back to get a better, more inclusive view of the tree. "You did it," she whispered, moved.

"*We* did it," Connor corrected. "You cut my work in half. Without you, I'd still be tugging the lights out of the box, trying to untangle them and doing my very best not to turn the air blue."

"You don't curse," she reminded him, denying his flippant assessment.

"Ha!" he laughed. "You haven't been around me after I spent three hours trying to put up strings of lights that just keep getting more tangled, not less."

He was just saying that to make her feel good, she thought. "I don't believe you."

"Well, thanks to you and your help, you'll never know," Connor told her. Blowing out a breath, he looked around the room. The floor was littered with empty boxes. "So what do you want to do?" he asked her. "Call it a night, or hang up a couple of decorations before turning in to grab a little sleep before your son decides he needs more attention?"

Her eyes met his. "What do you think?"

He saw the sparkle in her eyes, as well as the almost blinding smile on her lips. "I think I want to know what kind of vitamins you're taking and I want to get my hands on a supply."

"No vitamins," she denied. "I'm just really happy right now, that's all."

And she was. *Really* happy and that was all Connor's doing.

"Well, then, by all means, let's hang up a few decorations," he agreed. He loved seeing her like this. Loved the way she seemed to positively *shine*. He wanted to absorb the sight of that as much as he could.

A "few" decorations turned into a few more. And then a few more after that until all the ornaments she had taken out of their boxes earlier that day had found their place on the Christmas tree and there was absolutely nothing left to hang up.

"I guess the only thing that's left to do is clear away these boxes and store them up in the attic," Amy said. She looked around one more time to see if there were any more ornaments that she'd happened to overlook.

There weren't.

"I think *that* can wait until tomorrow," he told her with finality. He didn't mind decorating the tree, especially since it made her so happy. But cleanup was another story.

"Rita is *not* going to be okay with this mess when she comes in here in the morning."

"Rita likes to complain," Connor said. "It's her hobby. If she has nothing to complain about, then she *really* gets bent out of shape. Trust me, leaving all these empty boxes here like this gives the woman something to work with—literally." He smiled at Amy. "Consider it a public service."

"I never knew you had a bit of a lawyer in you," Amy said.

"No lawyer. I'm just someone who had to raise three scrappy kids while trying to keep a ranch going and earning some sort of a profit. You learn how to put out potential fires before they get started," he told her with a wink.

"You do have a lot of skills," Amy said with unabashed admiration.

Connor had no idea what possessed him to look down into her incredibly tempting, upturned face and murmur, "You have no idea."

Nor could he have said what spurred him on to do what he did next.

Because one minute they were just talking, shooting the breeze like two very old friends who knew one another well enough to finish each other's sentences, and then the next minute, somehow those same lips that were responsible for making those flippant quips had found their way to hers.

And just like that, with no warning, he was kissing her.

Kissing Amy the way he had always wanted to from perhaps the very first moment he had laid eyes on her all those years ago.

And the kiss turned out to be better than he'd thought it would be.

Way better.

It wasn't a case of just lips meeting lips; it was soul meeting soul.

Before Connor knew it, his arms had slipped around her, all but literally sweeping her off her feet and pulling her against him.

*Into* him.

The kiss deepened as he felt his pulse accelerating. He knew he shouldn't be doing this, not yet, not when she was still this vulnerable.

But despite his trying to talk himself out of it, it felt as if everything in his whole life had been leading to this very moment and it would somehow be against the natural order of things if he didn't at least allow himself to *enjoy* this for a single, shimmering moment in time.

CONNOR WAS KISSING HER.

*Oh my lord*, she thought, stunned. He was *kissing* her. And something inside of her didn't just respond to him; it *sang*.

Why hadn't he done that years ago? Amy silently demanded. Why hadn't he kissed her and made her realize that *he* was the one she was meant to be with, not Clay? And now it was too late, too late because she knew the type of man Connor was.

He was honorable to a fault.

He would think of her as Clay's wife, even if she was Clay's *ex*-wife.

Men like Connor didn't accept change easily and she had a feeling they didn't like thinking of themselves as being second choice. Even though the realization came to her, flying into her consciousness on a thunderbolt, that Connor wasn't second choice. Connor McCullough was the *only* choice and he always had been. She just hadn't known it until this very second because her brain had been numb and she hadn't been thinking.

Her heart was racing and her head was spinning so hard, Amy felt almost dizzy. Maybe that was why she wasn't thinking very clearly right now, but all she *could* think of was that she wanted to be with this man, be with him in every possible way.

Be with him *now*, before she lost her courage and before he came to his senses and did something noble, albeit hurtful, and pushed her away, murmuring something about not taking advantage of her.

Rising up on her toes, she wrapped her arms around Connor's neck and abandoned herself to the kiss, willing him to understand that it was all right if he took her now, that she wasn't about to push him away. That she *wanted* this with her whole heart and soul, possibly even far more than he did.

Amy felt him responding, felt Connor wanting her as his arms continued tightening around her. Felt her moment was at hand and she was more than ready to greet it head-on with open arms.

Felt that—

The small, plaintive cry pierced the still air, shattering the moment and throwing open the door to allow reality in all its less-than-gratifying regalia to push its way into the perfect world that had, for one brief shining moment, existed.

Jamie was crying. She could hear her son all the way down there.

She felt Connor's arms loosening from around her, felt his lips leaving hers. The actions ushered in a chill that all but froze her heart.

The moment, with all its promise of what could be, was gone.

"Jamie wants you," Connor murmured in a voice thick with all the emotion that he was struggling to shut down and away.

*And* I *want* you, Amy thought.

She knew she was being selfish, knew that of course the baby's needs came first and definitely before her own, but she could always diaper Jamie, and feed him, and rock him to sleep.

But what was happening here might very well never happen again, never have all the perfect conditions in place to happen again, and if she didn't snatch up her chance right here, right now, she might never—

Jamie's cries didn't subside. They grew a little louder, a little lustier in intensity, as if the baby sensed he needed to get her attention now, this moment, or she might not be able to come to him for a very long time.

With a sigh, attempting to collect herself, Amy stepped back from Connor. "It doesn't sound like he's going to stop."

"No," he agreed, his expression an unfathomable mask, "it doesn't."

"I'd better see what he needs," she said, doing her best not to sound as breathless as she felt at that moment.

"Do you need help?" Connor offered as she started to turn away and head toward the stairs.

She wanted to be able to pull herself together. Focusing on Jamie would help her do that.

"No, I can handle this," she told Connor. "Besides, it's late. You need to get your rest so you can get up early tomorrow to work."

Still, he remained standing where he was as she walked out of the living room. "Sure you don't want me in there?" Connor called after her.

"No, it's okay." *I don't want you there. I want you in my room, with me, making me realize what a fool I was to run off with Clay like that and leave Forever. To run off and leave you*, she added silently, really aching inside.

With a resigned sigh, Amy walked into the baby's room. The moment she did and saw the small, tearstained face looking up at her, she admonished herself.

She had no business ignoring Jamie, even for a second. No business aching to make love with Connor when she was first and foremost Jamie's mother and he needed her full, undivided attention.

"And you have it," she said out loud, reaching into the crib and picking him up. "You have *all* my attention because you are the world to me and you always will be. Mommy just lost her way for a second," she whispered. "But I'm back now and I'm back to stay. No worries, little man. You are the center of my universe. Now, let's get you changed so that *your* universe is a little drier, at least for a while."

Amy got busy, and as she did, she focused her thoughts on Jamie because he was all that mattered—and always would be.

## Chapter Thirteen

Amy shifted in the passenger seat of Connor's truck, trying to find a comfortable position for herself. It wasn't that she was really uncomfortable; she was just nervous. The truth was she always experienced nerves whenever she felt as if she was being judged or scrutinized.

Or going to be.

She had never been able to find that place of inner confidence the way that so many other young women did. She had never been able to shake that ugly-duckling feeling that she had two left feet, that she wasn't as pretty or as smart as all the other young women in town.

She supposed that was the reason she'd all but melted faster than a snowball in a desert in July when Clay had started paying attention to her. She simply could not get over the fact that someone as good-looking, as charming and magnetic as Clay, who could have his pick of any woman in Forever, was interested in someone like her.

So when Clay had crooked his finger in her direction and said *Let's go*, she'd done so without a single second's hesitation.

She should have hesitated, Amy thought regretfully, not for the first time since she'd gotten back.

As Connor pulled his truck into the parking lot right in front of Miss Joan's Diner, she felt her stomach tightening so hard that, for a moment, she couldn't manage to draw in a breath.

Connor slanted a look at her as he turned off the ignition.

"Amy, are you feeling all right?" he asked her, concerned. "You've lost all the color in your face."

Was she ill? He was tempted to touch her forehead to see if she was running a fever.

Amy drew in a big breath. There was no point in lying to Connor and telling him that everything was fine. If he were anyone else in the world, maybe she could pretend everything was fine, but she couldn't bring herself to lie, not to Connor, not even about little things.

"I feel like I'm eight years old again and bringing something to Miss Wright's class for show-and-tell," she told him with a self-conscious shrug. "Nothing I ever brought was good enough."

She expected him to look at her as if she'd lost her mind and laugh, dismissing her feelings.

Instead, Connor surprised her by saying, "Well, it was. And it *definitely* is now," he stressed. He reached for her hand, squeezing it. "There's no reason for you to be nervous. All Miss Joan wants to do is to meet this little guy. She likes to grumble and act like she spits out lead, but that lady is a pushover when it comes to babies. Tell you what. We can sit here until you feel up to going in and seeing her."

Amy flushed. "I guess that I'm being silly," she admitted.

"You can be anything you want after what you've been through," he said in a soothing, understanding voice. "But you know as well as I do that Miss Joan would be one of the first people to have your back if you ever feel like you need anything."

Amy pressed her lips together, nodding her head. "I know," she said, her voice so low it would have had to go up an octave to qualify as a whisper. Taking another breath, she centered herself, then nodded as she looked in Connor's direction. "Okay, I'm ready," she told him.

Getting out of the truck, he came around the hood to the passenger side and opened her door, taking her hand to help her out.

"Okay," he announced. "You wait right here and I'll get Jamie out of his car seat for you."

She had expressed surprise earlier to see that Connor had taken the car seat out of her vehicle and transferred it to his truck so that Jamie could be safely strapped in for his first official visit to Forever and Miss Joan's Diner.

"You think of everything," she marveled as he brought Jamie to her.

The baby was clutching on to the edge of his shirt, most likely getting it sticky, Amy thought. And miraculously, although he was aware of it, Connor didn't seem to mind.

"Except how to get you to stop feeling nervous," he commented.

A shy smile curved the corners of her mouth. "You've done a pretty good job with that, too," she said. "I'm about as calm as I'm ever going to be, walking into Miss Joan's Diner and having her judge me."

"Miss Joan doesn't judge," Connor gently reminded her. "She just looks at you and 'assesses' the situation." He placed the baby into her arms, then gently separated the small fingers from his shirt. Jamie mewled in protest. "You ready for this?" he asked Amy.

"As ready as I'll ever be," she answered, allowing her stomach to do one last flip-flop before she finally tightened her stomach muscles.

"Then let's go in and have you show this little guy off," Connor urged.

He took hold of the crook of her arm, helping to guide her up the steps to the diner's door. He held the door for her as Amy walked into the diner, carrying Jamie in her arms.

The conversation didn't instantly stop when she entered with her son, but to Amy it felt as if it had. She could have sworn that she was walking across the floor to the counter in what amounted to slow motion. If people *were* still talking, she couldn't make out any of the words. Not until she reached the counter and Miss Joan, who had shifted away from a customer and made her way to the exact spot where Amy would stop.

"Hello, Miss Joan," Amy said, the words feeling rather stiff and scratchy in her throat. She struggled hard not to feel like that insecure little girl again as she said, "This is my son, Jamie."

Sharp hazel-green eyes took complete measure of the child in Amy's arms in an instant. With a nod, Miss

Joan raised her head and directed her gaze at the baby's mother.

"Well, it certainly took you long enough to bring him in," Miss Joan said.

Connor immediately stepped up, interceding and deflecting the blame from Amy.

"That was my fault, Miss Joan. I was too busy with the ranch to bring her and Jamie into town."

Miss Joan glared at him. "She's not a side of beef that needs 'bringing in,' boy. Amy knows how to drive. She's been doing it since before she got her license, as I recall," the woman informed him, reminding Connor that she never forgot *anything*.

And then her eyes shifted back to the baby in Amy's arms.

Her voice softened. "What d'you say this handsome little guy's name was?" The question was meant for Amy, although Miss Joan never took her eyes off the baby.

"His name is Jamie," Amy answered, a sliver of pride entering her voice.

Miss Joan nodded in approval. "James," she said. "Good, strong name." She raised her eyes to Amy's. "You keep him on the right path, make sure he doesn't stray off it. You have any trouble, you bring him to me and I'll have a little talk with him."

Amy knew better than to demur or say that she wouldn't dream of bothering the woman with trivial things like instituting discipline when it came to her son. That was her job, one that she did feel qualified to take on. Knowing the difference between right and wrong wasn't all that hard.

So instead, Amy politely said "Yes, ma'am, I will" and

was rewarded with a quick nod of approval from the older woman.

"Why don't you get yourself a table, you three, and have some coffee and some of Angel's banana cream pie?" Miss Joan told them. "Angel just took it out of the oven less than half an hour ago." It was the closest Miss Joan came to coaxing. "You can have that, then go and help that baby of yours hang up his first ornament on the town Christmas tree." Anyone overhearing Miss Joan knew it was an order, not really a suggestion.

"But I already hung one up for him," Amy gently re- minded the woman.

"He wasn't here to watch you do that, now was he? Now he is," she replied simply, ending the discussion. "So, coffee and pie?" Her eyes swept over both of them even though their answers were a foregone conclusion.

"Coffee and pie," Amy echoed, knowing that Miss Joan meant well.

A small, pleased smile whispered along the older woman's lips.

"Coming right up," Miss Joan answered. Crossing to the window that was opened between the front of the diner and the kitchen, Miss Joan peered into the latter. "Angel, two slices of that banana cream pie of yours," she called to the attractive young woman in the white apron who seemed to be everywhere at once.

Satisfied that the order would be filled, Miss Joan went over to the urn to get the two cups of piping-hot coffee she'd promised.

In the interim, Amy and Connor went to the closest

empty table, a booth, and slid into the seats that were opposite one another.

"See?" Connor said, lowering his voice. "I told you that you were nervous for no reason. She's crazy about Jamie."

Amy wouldn't have exactly said Miss Joan was crazy about the baby. "How can you tell?" Amy asked him.

"Oh, I can tell," Connor assured her. "Besides," he pointed out, nodding at Jamie, "how could anyone resist that cute little face, those bright blue eyes and especially those chubby little cheeks?"

She couldn't help but think of Jamie's father. Except for once or twice in the very beginning, Clay's eyes had been flat and registered no emotion whatsoever whenever he looked at his son.

Rather than refer to Clay by name, Amy responded, "It could happen."

Connor shook his head. "Not in Miss Joan's case. She wouldn't have made such a big deal out of asking to see him if all she had intended to do was reject him. Trust me, that woman has a soft spot in her heart when it comes to kids."

Amy still seemed really tense, he thought. Leaning over the table between them, he lowered his voice again and told her, "Take a deep breath and relax, Amy. You're among friends. You have been ever since you came back to Forever."

Amy forced a smile to her lips before saying, "I know that."

The next moment, rather than send over one of the waitresses with the tray of two coffees and two plates of banana cream pie, Miss Joan brought the tray over to them herself.

"There you go," she said, setting the tray down on the table between them. And then she looked again at the infant in Amy's arms. "He seems like a happy baby," she pronounced. "Here's hoping nothing ever happens to make him lose that."

"We'll make sure of it," Connor assured her. And then he reached into his pocket and took out his wallet. "What do I owe you, Miss Joan?"

"The respect I'm due," the woman automatically replied. And then she said, "It's on the house. Merry Christmas, you two." The woman appeared to entertain a private thought, her eyes shifting from Connor to Amy. What looked like a ghost of a smile played along her thin lips for a moment. "It's about time," she murmured under her breath before she turned on her crepe heel and went back behind the counter.

"What did she just say?" Connor asked, turning toward Amy.

"'Merry Christmas, you two,'" Amy repeated.

Connor shook his head. "No, the other thing. After that."

Amy shrugged. She'd heard Miss Joan, but what the woman had said just raised more questions, questions Connor might not want to explore, so she pretended that she hadn't heard her.

"I didn't catch it," she told him.

Connor didn't want to let it go. "Something like 'it's about time,'" he said.

But Amy continued to play dumb. "I couldn't make

it out. It might have been that," she allowed, not wanting to discount the woman's words entirely.

But she had no desire to push them, either, because she didn't want Connor to feel as if he was being cornered, made to go along with something against his will.

Yes, he'd kissed her when they'd finished decorating the tree, but when Jamie cried, abruptly bringing an end to the intimacy, he had made no attempt to recapture that moment or even to say something about picking up where they had left off later. If he had been interested in her *at all* he would have said something to that effect, or at least *acted* as if he wanted to pick things up later.

Instead, the second what had been going on between them was forced to stop, *it had stopped*. Which to her meant that Connor wasn't all that into her or into there being something more, something meaningful between them.

Connor McCullough was her friend and that was where it stayed. Anything else was all in her mind.

And in her dreams.

But neither of that had any place in the real world. She needed to remember that and act like an adult, not a child waiting for Santa Claus to come down the chimney with a sack full of gifts.

Something was off.

Connor studied her face for a moment, trying to decide whether Amy was uncomfortable because of what Miss Joan had said, or if he was the one making her uncomfortable.

And if it was the latter, *why* was he making her uncomfortable?

He didn't recall feeling before that women were this complicated, but then, it had been a long time since he'd even had the time to contemplate things like that. The last time he'd even wondered about what made women tick was five years ago, when he'd found out Amy had run off with Clay Patton. That had happened less than a week after graduation and he remembered feeling completely crushed.

When Amy had turned up on his doorstep earlier this month, baby and all, he'd thought that despite the past, maybe he'd been given a second chance.

Now he wasn't so sure.

"You're awfully quiet," Amy noted.

For a second, Connor's mind went blank and he couldn't come up with a good excuse. "Just thinking," he finally told her.

"About work," she guessed, feeling guilty. "I took you away from the ranch. We could have come some other time."

"I'm not thinking about the ranch," he said. "And we came because Miss Joan wanted to see the baby—and I like keeping Miss Joan happy," he added. "She's kind of special to me."

*There*, he thought. *That should take the emphasis off Amy.*

"Think we can get Jamie to hold on to an ornament long enough to get him near enough to the tree?" he asked her.

"Maybe," she said, "but I really doubt that he's going to be able to hang an ornament on the tree."

Connor smiled. "He can if I help." And then he added, "If we can swing that, it'll make Miss Joan happy."

Amy didn't agree. "But Miss Joan's going to be in the diner. She won't know the difference."

Connor looked at her, wondering if Amy actually believed that. He felt he knew Miss Joan a little better than she did.

"Trust me, Amy, Miss Joan *always* knows the difference."

"Then we'd better go and see about finding a way to get Jamie to *hang* up that ornament," she said, sliding out of the booth.

Taking her son into her arms, she led the way out of the diner. They had an ornament to hang.

## Chapter Fourteen

Amy discovered that getting Jamie to hold an ornament in his hand was not a problem. Getting him to let go of that ornament, however, was.

When she found that she couldn't get her son to give up the Christmas ornament by trying to wiggle it out of his surprisingly tight grasp, she turned to Connor for help.

"Maybe you can get it out of that hot little hand of his," she said to Connor, temporarily giving up.

"I can try," Connor answered.

But his efforts were also unsuccessful because he didn't want to risk hurting the boy's hand. Jamie's fingers were tightly wrapped around the ornament, so much so that they seemed to almost be hermetically sealed around it.

"You know," Connor observed, "for a little guy, he's got one heck of a strong grip."

Amy hadn't wanted to risk the baby possibly cutting himself on an ornament, so she had deliberately gone through the decorations that were left in the boxes, looking for a small plastic one that Jamie could easily hold on to.

She'd finally found one lone reindeer—the other seven had to be hanging on the tree, she deduced—and pressed the figure into Jamie's little hand by carefully wrapping his fingers around it, one by one.

Obviously, she thought now, she'd done *too* good a job.

"Now what?" she asked Connor. "We can't take the ornament back to the ranch with us. It belongs on the tree."

Determined, she gave prying the reindeer out of her son's hand another try. She had the same lack of success. Jamie held fast to the ornament and this time he cried in protest when she tried to take it away from him.

Connor shook his head, almost impressed with the baby's tenacity.

"Well, he's too young to have a tantrum," Connor began.

Amy wasn't so sure. "How do you know he's too young to throw a tantrum?"

"After being around four babies, you pick up a few things," he said philosophically. Connor looked for a solution that didn't involve strong-arming the baby. "We can wait him out. He's bound to fall asleep. When he does, we'll just take the reindeer out of his hand and you can put it up for him. That's one solution."

"That might take a while," she pointed out. "And you can't just hang around here, waiting for Jamie to fall asleep. You've got a ranch to get back to."

The way he saw it, there was no real urgency to get

back. This was his slow season. "Cole's working the ranch. Once the horses are fed and watered, there's not that much to do right now," he said. "Most of the repairs have been taken care of."

He looked around the town square. "Besides, the weather's crisp, but not that numbing kind of cold it can be. It's the kind of day that makes a man glad he's alive."

*And spending it with you*, he added silently, slanting a glance in her direction.

Amy smiled. He was saying that for her benefit, she thought, so she wouldn't feel bad about this. "You really are a good guy, Connor McCullough."

Connor watched as the winter sun seemed to shimmer and dance in her hair, making him remember so many random moments from the past. Moments that had been filled with adolescent hope and dreams of tomorrow.

"You wouldn't say that if you knew what I was thinking," he said.

For one brief moment, as his eyes met hers, she felt her pulse begin to race. She told herself she was imagining it, but something in her heart told her that she *knew* what he was thinking. And maybe what he was thinking was only meant to last for a little while—a quick Christmas fling with an old friend—but she didn't care. She just hoped she was right because if she was, she would take whatever she could get if it meant that they could be together.

And that in turn meant she needed to get Connor home so this could play out in private.

She searched for a solution, and suddenly, inspiration

hit her. Holding Jamie close against her, Amy began to walk fast.

"Where are you going?" Connor asked, quickly falling into step beside her.

"I need to sit down," she said as she picked up her pace. She was heading toward the general store.

There were two rather weather-beaten benches out in front of the store. They'd been there for as long as anyone could remember. Some of Forever's senior residents liked to sit there, watching the rest of the town going about their business and commenting on them.

Most days, there were at least three, sometimes four and on occasion five, older citizens sitting there, observing the rest of the town going to and from the general store and the attached hardware store.

All Amy needed was a small space for a couple of minutes. Three at best.

Connor still wasn't clear why she was heading toward the bench.

"Do you need to change him?" Connor asked. If she did, they'd left the bag with Jamie's diapers, as well as his bottle, in the truck. "I can go back to the truck—" he started to offer.

Amy cut him off. "No, I don't need to change him. I need to make him laugh."

Connor looked at her, totally puzzled. That made no sense to him and he told Amy as much.

"I don't understand."

Amy flashed him a smile. "You will" was all she said.

Reaching the benches that were in front of the general store, she found a space on the second one. Planting herself down on the bench, she glanced at the two men already sitting there. Quite possibly, they'd been there since early morning.

"Hope you gentlemen don't mind," she said.

"Mind? You're the nicest thing to happen to this bench in a long time," Jethro Wilkins, eighty-three years young and a onetime would-be rodeo star, told her as he moved closer to his seatmate to give her room.

"Cute little young'un," his seatmate, Calvin Dobbs, commented. He pointed to the reindeer clutched in Jamie's hand. "Looks like he's caught himself one of Miss Joan's decorations."

"Not for long," Amy said. Settling Jamie onto her lap, she kept him supported with one arm while with her free hand, she tugged his jacket and shirt up, exposing his round little belly.

Before Connor could ask her what she was up to, Amy leaned forward, and with her lips pressed to her son's belly, she began to blow against it, tickling Jamie. Jamie started to laugh. It was a full belly laugh that gladdened the hearts of everyone within a small radius who had the pleasure of hearing the heartwarming sound.

The second she started tickling her son, Connor realized what she was up to. Laughing, Jamie soon loosened his childish grip on the ornament and Connor was able to work the reindeer out of his hand.

"Got it," he declared.

The moment he did, Amy lifted her lips away from her son's tummy. Jamie giggled for a second or two longer, and then the sound slowly subsided. The large blue eyes seemed to look right at her with wonder, as if to ask "What happened?"

"Sorry, little guy. If you weren't going to hang it up, the reindeer had to go back into the box," Amy told her son.

Jamie's gaze shifted to his hand and he opened and closed his little fist, staring at it.

Watching him, Connor laughed. "I think he realizes something is missing."

"I think you're right," Amy agreed. "Sorry, sweetie," she told her son. "You had your chance." Turning toward Connor, she nodded at the ornament he had in his hand. "Why don't you hang it up for him and then we can get back to the ranch?"

"You leaving so soon?" Jethro asked. The old-timer clearly looked disappointed to have Amy and the baby go.

"Just for now," Amy answered, giving the older man a smile. "Jamie needs his nap."

Jethro's bench mate nodded. "Yeah. Come to think of it," Calvin said, slowly getting up to his feet, "I could use one myself."

"You're *always* napping," Jethro grumbled. Reluctantly, the other man got up off the bench as well, using the bench's armrest for leverage to boost him to his feet.

"See you gentlemen around," Amy said, nodding at them. Leaving, Amy met Connor halfway as he returned from hanging up Jamie's reindeer on the tree.

"We don't have to leave if you don't want to go just yet," he said the moment she reached him.

Her eyes met his just the way they had a few minutes

ago and she saw the same thing in them now as she had then. Something that told her that this evening was going to be different from other evenings. She had a feeling that what had been hinted at with that kiss after they'd finished decorating Connor's Christmas tree just might, given half a chance, finally reach its fruition.

But she'd never find out if it could by just standing around here in town or sitting in Miss Joan's Diner.

"Oh, but I do want to go back to the ranch," she told him in all seriousness.

Was it his imagination, or was she covertly saying what he was hoping she was saying?

Or maybe he wanted it so much, he was reading things into everything she was saying? That was a definite possibility, he thought.

But she did say she wanted to go back to the ranch, so he could act on at least that part of it.

After that, he'd play it by ear.

"Okay, then, let's go home." And then he thought of something. "Do you want to stop at Miss Joan's Diner and let her know that we wound up hanging up Jamie's ornament for him?"

"No need," Amy answered. "She's Miss Joan. She'll know. Your words, remember?"

Connor grinned, nodding his head. "My words." He glanced at the baby in her arms as they turned in the general direction of the diner's parking lot and his truck. "Looks like he's falling asleep."

"I guess laughing like that took a lot out of a little guy," Amy commented.

"I guess," he echoed. And then the corners of his

mouth curved again. "Looks like your little guy's got good timing."

"We'll see," she said.

JAMIE SLEPT ALL the way back to the ranch.

As if on cue, he woke up the moment Connor pulled his truck up in front of the house.

"It's like he knows he's home," Connor noted, turning off the ignition. He got out of the truck and came around to the rear passenger seat. He watched as Amy took her son out of the car seat.

*Home.*

As in *their* home, Amy thought, dwelling on the word he'd just used.

Was that just a slip on his part or had Connor made the reference without giving it any thought?

There was the outside chance that he had used the word deliberately, that he considered his home *her* home as well, but she felt that was too much to hope for.

Most likely it had just been a slip, but she really did want to believe, just for a moment, that he had meant it the way it sounded. That this was *her* home, too. Hers and Jamie's.

And if she'd only realized the kind of man Connor was, the kind of qualities he possessed—good, kind, long-lasting qualities that were steadfast rather than the kind that dissolved like a pile of sugar left out in the rain—then maybe this *would have* already been her home rather than just a place where she hoped she'd find a little refuge until she could figure out what to do with the rest of her life.

Hers and Jamie's, she amended.

"You're not going to remember any of this," Connor was telling the baby. "But trust me, this is going to make for a good story, and in a couple of years, you're going to be telling this to people as if you recalled every second of it yourself."

"You're talking to him as if he understands you," Amy said.

She went to take Jamie from him, but Connor had already started to walk to the front door, holding the baby as if doing so was something he was very comfortable with.

"That's because he does," Connor told her simply. "He understands every single word."

She looked at Connor skeptically. "No, he doesn't."

She believed that babies Jamie's age responded to sounds and cadence, not words.

But it was obvious that Connor had a completely different view of the situation.

"From the moment they come into the world, babies are like tiny little sponges, absorbing everything they hear, every single word. Make no mistake about it," Connor assured her.

Amy laughed softly, shaking her head. "You really believe that?" she asked, following Connor and her son to the front door.

Connor didn't hesitate for a moment. "Absolutely," he told her.

"Well, then, I guess it must be true." Amy looked at her son. "Right, Jamie?" she asked.

"Right, Mom," Connor answered in a high-pitched

voice pretending to be Jamie. "Uncle Connor always knows what he's talking about."

The high-pitched voice was so completely out of character for Connor that Amy just started to laugh. Really laugh. She laughed all the way into the house and continued to laugh so hard, she wound up with tears rolling down her cheeks.

Her laughter brought Rita hurrying into the room. "Is something wrong?" she asked, concerned, looking from Amy to Connor.

"Nothing's wrong, Rita. Miss Amy just found something that I said to be very funny," he told the housekeeper, omitting the part that mentioned he had said it in a high-pitched voice, pretending to be a precocious six-month-old. "She was laughing."

"Oh. I thought she was crying. From the kitchen, it is hard to tell the difference. Laughter is a good sound," she pronounced. Rather than return to the kitchen, Rita took the baby from Connor. "How did he like his first trip into town?" she asked them. Before either one of them could answer her, Rita looked down at the baby and noted that his long lashes were beginning to droop again. "It looks like all that fresh air has tired him out."

"He slept in the truck. Isn't it too soon for him to be falling asleep again?" Amy asked, slightly concerned. It was winter. Maybe Jamie was catching a cold or coming down with something.

"Babies sleep when they want to. They wake up when they want to, too," Rita replied, unfazed by the note of concern in Amy's voice. "I suggest that you do whatever you need to do now because later, you may not be able to. Babies do not go by the same clock that we do," the housekeeper said matter-of-factly.

Connor glanced out the large front window. It looked out on the stables in the distance.

"Did Cole come by the house?" he asked Rita.

Rita knew what he was asking her. "He did not come in to say he was leaving."

Which meant that Cole was still here, he thought. "Then maybe I'd better check on him," Connor said, heading back toward the front door.

Amy had the distinct impression that he was saying that to her rather than to Rita.

"I'll put the baby down for a nap and then help Rita with dinner," she told him.

Rita relinquished her hold on the baby, handing him over to his mother.

"Rita, the housekeeper," she informed her, "does not need help with dinner."

Amy bit her lip. "I didn't mean to insult you," she said.

"You did not," Rita replied as she retreated to the kitchen.

Amy sighed. Finding her proper rhythm in this household was going to take time, she thought, but she wasn't about to give up trying.

# *Chapter Fifteen*

Amy kept looking at the clock on the far living room wall so often, she was sure its hands had somehow frozen in place. Or at the very least, something had happened to the mechanism to cause the clock to move slower than molasses in January. So when she heard the front door open, she jumped to her feet, startled and relieved at the same time. Connor was finally back. It was only extreme control that kept her from rushing over to him.

Instead, as calmly as she could, Amy said, "I thought maybe you weren't going to come in tonight."

The sun had gone down over two hours ago. It was dark outside and past seven. What she had really thought was that she'd done something to scare Connor off and he'd decided to spend the night in the stable, choosing the company of horses over hers.

Connor looked at her, confused.

"Why would you think that?" He shrugged out of his sheepskin-lined jacket as if he were shedding something that weighed a ton. Trying to move fast, he'd accidentally gotten his jacket wet and the lining had swelled, doubling its weight. "I felt bad about leaving Cole with all the work while I was in town, so I told him to go home to Stacy and the twins, and I took care of bedding down the horses for the night," he explained. "How was dinner?"

"Good, I imagine. I wouldn't know firsthand because I haven't had any."

Draping his jacket on a hook by the door, Connor looked at her quizzically.

"Rita's not very happy with me," Amy admitted, "but I told her I wanted to wait for you before I ate dinner. I think she went to her room, grumbling under her breath, something about working for people who had no sense of order."

"You should have gone ahead and had dinner without me," Connor told her and then guessed, "You must be starving."

"No more than you, probably. C'mon," she urged, turning to lead the way to the kitchen. "I'll warm dinner up. Knowing Rita, she probably left it on the stove for us. Well, for you," she amended, then laughed. "I think she'd be happier if I just foraged for food out in the forest whenever I wanted to eat."

"You know that's not true," Connor protested, walking into the kitchen. "Rita likes you."

Maybe she was being too sensitive, Amy thought. That was a holdover from the number Clay had done on her self-esteem. If it could even still be called *self-esteem*. Right now, it had the consistency of shredded wet newspapers.

As to the matter of Rita, she was willing to be persuaded.

"How can you tell?" she asked.

"Oh, I can tell," Connor assured her. "Rita doesn't stand on ceremony. She'll tell you exactly what she thinks. She feels that at her age, she's earned the right to show her displeasure—without any reservations—if that's what she's feeling."

The second he walked into the kitchen he was confronted with the enticing, very pleasing aroma of what Rita had prepared for dinner: roasted pork loin, plus baby red potatoes and green beans. The combined scent hung in the air, creating its own seductive perfume.

"How could you not have given in and had dinner?" he asked.

"I told you, I was waiting for you." Amy pointed toward the table. "Sit. I'll bring the food over to the table."

Connor did as she asked and sank down in the closest chair. He was pretty tired. Maybe that was why he was giving in so easily.

"You know," he stressed one last time, "you didn't have to wait for me to come in." He definitely didn't want her to feel that she was obligated to wait until he could join her at the table before eating. "You could have had your dinner when it was ready."

"It's no fun eating alone," she told him. For a second, a glimmer of sadness crossed her face as she thought back over the last five years. "I've had too many meals alone."

Moving quickly, she set out the pork loin then got serving bowls for both the baby red potatoes and the serving of breadcrumb-covered green beans.

"What would you like to drink?" she asked, opening the refrigerator. Looking, she zeroed in on the first beverage she saw. "Do you want beer?"

"That sounds good," he said, although he would have said the same thing no matter what she would have suggested. He just wanted her taking a seat at the table. "Come sit down," Connor urged. "You don't have to wait on me."

"And you didn't have to take me into town today," she pointed out, slipping into the chair opposite his. "Or go through all that trouble to bring that Christmas tree into the house."

He didn't want her thanking him. What he did for her he did because he wanted to do it. Because he wanted to do something for *her*.

"Well, full disclosure," he said, clearing his throat as he began to help himself to dinner. "I do get a tree every year."

She knew that, but she also knew something else. "Yes, but Cole said that you don't usually get one this early. And he also told me that you were thinking of *not* getting one this year." She put a serving of pork, as well as a large spoonful of potatoes and one of the green beans, onto her own plate.

Connor waved away her report of his brother's words. "Cole just likes to hear himself talk. Don't pay attention to anything he says—he's been known to make things up as he goes along."

Amy watched him for a long moment. Connor seemed like he was protesting too much.

"So, you *didn't* get that Christmas tree early because Jamie and I were here?" she asked.

Connor shifted in his chair, making eye contact with his green beans and not her. "Well, I wouldn't exactly say that," he qualified, casting about for a safe way to get out of this conversation and shift it in another direction.

Amy saw right through him and grinned. "I would," she told him. "And I'd also say that that was very sweet of you."

Connor shrugged, still uncomfortable with the altruistic light she was shining on him. "I don't know about 'sweet,' but I do know that you deserve to have something nice done for you."

He paused for a moment, pretending to focus on his dinner when he was trying to find a way to properly frame his question without hurting her feelings—or her pride.

At a loss as to how to proceed, he finally just plunged in and said, "Do you mind if I ask you a question?"

Her automatic response was to say yes, she did mind. Questions usually just brought her failings front and center. But she knew that the only way she and Connor were ever going to get permanently back to the level of easy friendship they had once enjoyed was if she didn't keep withdrawing into the protective shell she had built up around herself. This was Connor talking to her, not Clay. He wasn't trying to trap her and there was no reason for her to be leery.

"Go ahead," she told Connor. "Ask."

His eyes held hers. "Why did you stay with Clay so long?" He wanted to word his question differently, more sharply, but he didn't want to take a chance on accidentally inflicting any more pain on Amy than she'd already suffered through.

Amy shrugged, lowering her eyes and looking at what was left of her dinner. "I kept hoping it would get better."

"And when it didn't?" he gently prodded, instinctively knowing that it hadn't. That there hadn't been any good days to offset the bad ones, as in normal relationships. Clay Patton was a raging narcissist. A narcissist didn't see anyone or anything beyond his own boundaries. His world was comprised of a population of one: himself.

Clay was the only one who mattered to Clay and it killed Connor that she had been drawn into this self-esteem-stifling world where Clay had done everything in his power to rob her of her individuality—and that winsome smile he'd come to love so much.

"And when it didn't," Amy repeated quietly, "I was too embarrassed to admit it. Besides, my dad was dead and my mother was starting a new life with my step-father in another state. I tried to stick it out with Clay because I didn't have anywhere else to go."

"You *always* had somewhere to go," Connor told her pointedly. "And you did. You came here."

She had, but that was out of a sense of desperation. "But I didn't want to," she confessed. When he looked at her sharply, she explained, "I didn't want to admit, even silently, that I'd failed."

She had the wrong take on the situation, Connor thought. "You didn't fail, Amy," he told her with feeling. "*Clay* did."

Of course he'd say that. That was the kind of person Connor was. "You're just being very kind, Connor," she said.

"No," he contradicted. "I'm just seeing it the way it really is. I know you," he emphasized. "You did your best in this situation. Clay didn't have a 'best' to bring to the game."

Finished eating, Connor pushed his plate back on the table as he looked at her. Thinking of the way Clay had treated Amy had gotten him so angry, he'd forgotten to hold his tongue, and consequently, he'd overstepped his bounds.

"Look, I'm sorry, Amy," he apologized. "I didn't mean to open up old wounds."

"Don't be sorry, Connor," she said. She didn't want him to feel he had to censor himself when he talked to her. She appreciated his passion—and that he was on her side. Picking up the empty dinner plates and utensils, she brought them over to the sink and began filling it with hot, sudsy water. "You took me in and quite possibly saved my life. You saved Jamie's. You can ask me anything you want."

"Okay," Connor said, taking her up on what she had just said. "Then can I ask you not to do the dishes?" he said, nodding toward the sink.

Amy laughed. She should have known he'd say something like that.

"There is no way I'm leaving dirty dishes in the sink for Rita to find in the morning. I do that and she'll have my head gift-boxed and sent off to the dead letter office."

He pretended to take her protest seriously. "I don't think they have that anymore."

She had no idea if they did or not; she just remembered hearing about it a long time ago.

"In Rita's case, they'd resurrect it for her," she laughed. "Besides, this is no big deal." Amy scrubbed a dish, then rinsed it before setting it on the rack to dry. "See? One down already. This'll only take a few minutes."

There was no talking her out of it and he knew it. So Connor got up and joined her at the sink.

"It'll take less time if there're two of us doing it," he said.

He'd brought his bottle of beer with him and now took a short swig before putting the bottle down on the counter. He intended to sink his hands into the sudsy water but Amy's next move prevented him from doing that.

She'd turned abruptly to argue with him, wanting to get him to go sit back down again. At the very least, doing the dishes was her small attempt to pay him back in some way. To her thinking, keeping the peace with Rita was a good way to start.

But when she turned to make her point and get him to sit down again, she found that he was standing a little too close to avoid her bumping up against him. The sudden, unexpected contact was jolting and she sucked in her breath in surprise.

"I need a bigger kitchen," Connor quipped, grabbing hold of her shoulders to keep her from falling. And then he looked down into her face. "On second thought," he quietly murmured as an impulse took hold of him, "maybe the kitchen is just the right size."

The next moment, as he continued to hold on to her shoulders, the impulse that had come over him won.

He brought his mouth down to hers and kissed her.

He knew he should stop. Knew a great many things logically. But emotionally, well, emotionally, given this time and this place, it was the right thing to do.

The *only* thing to do because the moment he kissed her, the hunger in his soul flowered and took over every corner of his being, declaring that it wouldn't be satisfied until he did this.

Before he could stop himself, the kiss continued. Continued and wove itself into the very fiber of his being, going on to weave itself into every part of him. And making him crave more.

It took every ounce of his strength to put the skids on what was almost happening. What he couldn't allow to happen, much as he wanted it to.

WHEN HE DREW BACK, Amy looked up at him, dazed and stunned. Was he rejecting her? Had he suddenly realized that he didn't want what she had to offer?

She knew she should just accept what was happening and withdraw, but she felt so hurt, she couldn't retreat meekly. Clay had rejected her time and again, pushing her physically away, but this was Connor. Connor wouldn't do that.

Would he?

"Did I do something wrong?" she asked him.

"What?" For a moment, he thought he hadn't heard her correctly. And then he answered, "No, no, you didn't. But I almost did."

She kept telling herself to back away, but somehow,

she just couldn't. She had to know *why* he was rejecting her. "By making love with me?" she asked.

"Yes."

"Do you find me that off-putting?" she asked, fighting back tears.

He looked at her as if she had suddenly lost her mind. "No, of course not."

"Then why did you just pull away from me as if I had some kind of awful disease? Because I don't," she quickly assured him, wondering if she'd suddenly stumbled across the reason he was treating her as if she had leprosy or something equally as awful.

"I didn't pull away from you because of something I thought you had," he told her, moving away from her.

"Oh. Then you're just not attracted to me."

"Oh God, no. Just the opposite. I'm *too* attracted to you," he said.

The frustration he was experiencing made him start to pace around the kitchen.

She stared at him, thoroughly confused. "You're not making any sense, Connor."

"Try looking at it from my perspective," he said with a disparaging laugh.

"Okay. Then explain it to me," she said. "Make me understand why, if you're attracted to me like you just said you are, why you don't want to kiss me."

"I do."

She took a deep breath, plunging in. "Or make love with me."

"That's just it," he told her almost helplessly. "I do."

"Then what's the problem?" she cried, totally at a loss as to why they were at an impasse.

"The problem is that you're vulnerable and hurt, and if I pressure you into making love with me, you might never forgive me. And then any chance we might have for something to develop between us will die."

Amy stared at him, trying to absorb what Connor was saying. "You're serious?"

"Yes," Connor replied even though this was killing him.

"Connor, you would *never* pressure me," she said. "And what makes you think I don't want this?"

"You don't want this," he insisted. "You're not thinking clearly."

"You might be smarter than I am," she allowed, remembering how well Connor had always done in high school. "But you are dead wrong. I am thinking very clearly and I have never wanted anything more in my whole life."

He looked at her, his heart all but stopping. "You're sure?"

"Very, very sure," she told him in a low, soft whisper.

"Good enough for me," he replied, sweeping her up into his arms the next moment. He began to walk to the stairs.

She linked her arms around his neck. "Where are we going?"

"I'd love to take you someplace exotic," he said, "but you'll have to settle for my room."

She smiled up into his eyes. "What makes you think that's not exotic?"

He kissed her then. Kissed her long and hard, causing time to temporarily stand still. "Exotic enough for you?" he asked as he began to walk up the stairs.

There was mischief in her eyes as she replied, "It's a start."

"Brace yourself for act two," he whispered.

Her heart was pounding madly as her imagination took flight. It was finally happening.

"Braced and ready to go," she told him in a hushed whisper.

Connor picked up his pace.

## Chapter Sixteen

Connor's room was only two doors down from Jamie's bedroom. As he brought Amy to his bedroom, Connor sincerely hoped that the baby would continue sleeping, at least for the next hour. With all his heart, he wanted to make love with Amy.

But if the baby started to cry, Connor was certain that he would be able to hear him. He was not about to put his own needs, demanding though they were, above Jamie's, or those of Jamie's mother—and she would always be Jamie's mother first and foremost.

Connor mentally crossed his fingers.

The moment Connor was inside his room, he pushed the door closed with the back of his elbow. There was no need to lock the door. The closed door afforded him all the privacy he needed. There was no one else in the ranch house, other than his housekeeper, and she was in her room downstairs.

Rita would never walk into his room if she needed something. At the very most, the woman would knock on his door. So for all intents and purposes, he and Amy were alone. And now that he had Amy's full consent, he intended to act on his feelings, the feelings he had been harboring inside himself for such a very long time.

Lips still sealed to Amy's, Connor set her down, letting her feet touch the floor.

As he slowly slid her down out of his arms, he held her close to him. So close that their heartbeats seemed to strike a rhythm, beating almost as if they were one.

Feeling her heart against his aroused Connor even more. He wanted her so much that it literally hurt, but even so, he held himself in check. Instinct told him that Clay had been a rough, demanding lover, and he did *not* want to do anything that would even vaguely remind Amy of the man she had run away from.

So Connor made love to her slowly, lyrically, causing every part of her to hum with anticipation. He made sure that every part of her would feel cherished and adored because she deserved that.

That and so much more.

Kissing Amy with reverence, his lips slowly moved from hers, lingering on her cheeks, her eyes, then the hollow of her throat.

Her sharp intake of breath made him go even slower to make sure that he left an imprint on her soul.

CONNOR CAUSED HER blood to rush the instant his lips traced a path from one side of her neck to the other. Her breath became shorter and shorter as her anticipation steadily grew, blossoming to huge proportions.

Though she couldn't remember just how, Amy suddenly found herself with her back pressed against his bed as zippers and buttons were being parted and her clothes were slowly being peeled away, one inch at a time, until they eventually ceased to be barriers between them.

Her desire grew more and more intense as her anticipation continued to increase, reaching tremendous proportions. For the first time, Amy understood what lovemaking—and the hunger associated with it—was all about.

She had never felt like this before, never had eagerness seize her like this, gripping her and holding her fast as she desperately ached for, and sought, fulfillment... that final starburst of energy that she had only heard about but never experienced.

Impatient in her enthusiasm, she almost ripped Connor's shirt and pulled frantically at his jeans until they were no longer in the way.

Her zeal seemed to completely overwhelm him as she sought to find a way to make Connor feel at least a little of the wondrous sensation that she was experiencing right then.

She was confident that he was well versed in lovemaking, but she felt like a complete novice, coming to the table with no real notion of what it felt like to be wanted for who and what she was.

With Clay, she had quickly been made to feel that she had only been an interchangeable entity and anyone could have been in her place instead of her.

Connor made her feel precious.

And desired.

AMY BECAME ALMOST FRENZIED. Catching her wrist to anchor her to the moment, Connor looked at her, stunned by this insatiable, incredible creature in his arms.

"Amy?"

Dazed, she stopped for a moment and looked up at him. "Something wrong?"

Connor found the sound of her voice reassuring. The smile he gave her in response went from his lips to his eyes and down into his very soul. A soul he now offered to her.

"No, nothing's wrong. Nothing at all." As far as he was concerned, everything was right between them, as well as right with the world.

A fire burned within him as he covered her with hot, hungry kisses. He worked his way from one end of her body to the other, branding all of her and making Amy indelibly his for as long as they both lived.

He wanted to bring her as much pleasure as he could because just being with her brought him a feeling of indescribable well-being.

Using his hands, his lips, his tongue, Connor expertly brought her to one climax, then another.

Each time she cried his name, it fed his desire to bring her up again and he did. Did it several times over until she all but sank back into his bed, on the very fringe of exhaustion.

Satisfied that he had pleasured her as much as he possibly could, Connor drew himself up slowly over the length of her body until his eyes were just above hers, his body covering hers.

Bringing his mouth down on hers again, he entered her, sealing their bodies together.

Passion rushed through his veins as he began to move his hips. He could tell that each movement fueled her desire as well as his own.

He found himself going faster every fraction of a moment until the tempo turned from a slow dance to a race undertaken at breakneck speed.

Locked in each other's arms, they continued the race to the very top of the summit, then plunged down together amid a shower of sparks that had caused desire to burst into flames.

Enraptured, Amy had to bite down on her lip to keep from crying out his name. She didn't want to wake the baby—or risk being heard by the housekeeper. But inside of her, everything was shouting for joy. What she was feeling was nothing short of spectacular, and the sensation had created a feeling that was so incredibly special, it made tears spring to her eyes.

Tears that left their imprint on Connor.

Concerned, he raised himself up on his elbow and peered down into her face, searching for answers to questions that were only half-formed.

"Amy?"

Dizzy, her head spinning, she struggled to focus on the sound of his voice. Everything else was a million miles away. "Hmm?"

"Amy, did I hurt you?" Connor asked, really concerned now that he had.

Her eyes were closed. Opening them, she raised her

hand and pressed her index finger against Connor's lips, silencing him.

"Shh. I might have died and gone to heaven, so I can't give you a complete answer yet," she replied.

Sincerely worried now and wondering if she had become delirious, Connor tried again. "Amy, I don't think that I understand—"

Amy smiled, still clinging for all she was worth to the out-of-body feeling she had just experienced. "Connor," she whispered, "you're talking through the most wonderful experience of my life."

He was doing his best to understand what she was telling him. "Then you're okay?" he asked her uncertainly.

"Oh, I am *so* much better than okay," she told him, struggling not to giggle.

Amy's smile was radiant as she looked up at him again, and then, without warning, she pulled his face down to hers and kissed him.

It was a long, languid kiss, filled with feeling and ending with a heartfelt, happy sigh.

"But you were crying," Connor pointed out, thoroughly confused.

"Tears of joy, Connor," she said. "Those were tears of joy."

Connor shook his head. "I am *never* going to understand that," he said, unable to reconcile the two feelings. Just how could someone be happy and yet be crying at the same time? It made absolutely no sense to him.

"That's okay," Amy murmured. "You don't have to."

Utterly contented, she curled her body into his, wanting to live in the moment for as long as she possibly could.

"I never knew it could be like this," she confessed, then added, in case he hadn't figured it out, "It was pretty amazing."

Connor's arm tightened around her and he pulled her closer to him. Kissing the top of her head, he felt an overwhelming wave of affection totally drenching him.

"And you are pretty amazing yourself," Connor told her.

She raised her head so she could look up at him. "Me?"

"Don't see anybody else here with me," he said. "Of course you. You are a beautiful, amazing woman and it's about time that you realized it." He punctuated each sentence with a kiss.

Her eyes were smiling at him as she said, "You don't need to make me feel good."

"No, I don't," he agreed. "But I do like telling the truth and that's what I just did. I told you the truth. You are amazing."

Amy couldn't bring herself to believe that. "But—" she began to protest.

This time, he was the one who placed his finger against her lips.

"No 'but.' You are an amazing, beautiful woman. End of story. On second thought," he said, reconsidering, "*not* end of story." He enfolded her even more tightly in his arms. "Beginning of story."

She didn't understand what he was trying to tell her.

Or maybe she was afraid to. She'd already had too many hopes dashed.

"Beginning?" Amy questioned.

"Beginning," Connor repeated.

Her breath caught in her throat as warm sensations bathed her all over again. He made her feel wanted, something she'd never once felt with Clay. He'd made sure of that.

"Does that mean you want to make love with me?" she asked hopefully.

Connor grinned broadly, tickled by her innocence. "What do you think?"

Her smile rose from her lips into her eyes. "I think we should stop talking and get to it before the baby wakes up."

Connor said nothing in reply. His lips were far too busy with hers.

THE SECOND TIME was even better than the first. She didn't think that it was humanly possible, but it was. Connor was such a gentle, incredibly considerate lover, she thought that she might have imagined what had happened the first time around.

But when he behaved in the same manner the second time, Amy realized that this was the way Connor really was: a gentle, kind lover who knew how to make her heart—and every other part of her—sing.

And that somehow, for whatever reason, she had turned out to be very, very lucky to have someone like Connor in her life.

He made her feel safe and protected.

And very, very happy.

She knew that she couldn't expect this to go on forever, that this was just an interlude in her life, a beautiful, beautiful interlude, but still temporary nonetheless.

She'd had enough disappointments in her life to know that she couldn't set her heart on anything. Happily-ever-after was for other women, but not for her. Clay had proved that to her over and over again. She had kept hoping he'd change and mentally she'd given him chance after chance to do so—and he never once did. *She* was the problem, not him, he'd told her more than once.

So, thinking that she had finally found the man of her dreams was incredibly naive and foolish, and she told herself that she really knew better than that.

It was just her heart that secretly hoped she was right, that somehow, she and Connor not only were meant to be together, but really *would* be together until the end of their days.

*Right*, she thought, silently mocking herself. And the first moment she breathed anything close to that to him, Connor would suddenly tell her, albeit politely, that she and Jamie had overstayed their welcome.

And right after that, he would run for the hills as quickly as he could.

But all that was later. And right now, she had this, an incredible experience to hold in her heart and relive until it was completely frayed and in tatters.

AMY DIDN'T REMEMBER falling asleep.

She'd had so much on her mind, she was certain she would keep herself up until dawn finally pushed its way into the room. But she must have fallen asleep because the next thing she knew, she was opening her eyes and waking up.

And finding that she was alone in Connor's bed.

Puzzled and confused, Amy sat up and looked around, but Connor was nowhere in the room.

She thought for a moment that he might have needed to use the bathroom, but the bathroom door was wide-open and there was no light coming from it.

He wasn't there.

"Good job, Amy," she murmured under her breath. "You managed to actually make the man flee his own bed just to get away from you."

Why else would he be gone?

Amy sighed as she dragged her hand through her hair. She knew what she and Connor had wasn't destined to go on forever, but she'd actually thought it would last longer than just the span of one night.

Not even a whole night, at that.

Well, there was no use mourning the demise of something that never was, Amy told herself, refusing to let her emotions get the better of her.

Getting out of bed, Amy quickly collected her clothes from the floor. She put them on as fast as she could, wanting to slip out of Connor's room before Rita showed up in the hall for some reason and saw her. Explaining why she was leaving Connor's room in the middle of the night would be very awkward.

*Stop thinking about yourself. You have a son to take care of, remember?* Amy upbraided herself.

Jamie only slept a few hours at a clip and this was

way longer than he normally slept. For some reason, to-night he hadn't cried and woken her up—

What if he had cried and she'd just slept through it? she suddenly thought. What kind of a mother ignored her own baby because she was exhausted after making love for half the night?

*A bad one*, Amy silently said, answering her own rhetorical question.

*Nothing* should come before Jamie, she told herself angrily.

Opening the bedroom door slowly, she looked around to make sure she was alone. Relieved, she slipped out and closed the door behind her.

With her heart lodged in her throat, Amy hurried down the hall past her own room until she reached Jamie's. She had no idea what she expected to find once she went in, but she was hoping for the best.

Turning the doorknob very slowly in case he was still asleep, she eased the door open and peered into the bedroom.

What she saw made her mouth drop open.

Connor was there, sitting in the rocking chair he'd moved into the room for her when they'd brought the crib in. He was holding Jamie in his arms, and from his body language, he had apparently just rocked the baby to sleep.

As if sensing her presence, Connor looked over his shoulder in her direction.

"Go back to bed," he told her in a whisper. "I have this."

What he had, Amy thought as she watched him, was her heart—utterly and completely.

## Chapter Seventeen

Amy would have been the first to admit that over the last few years, she had come to expect the worst to happen. To wait for it to rise up and engulf her, wrapping up her heart in despair.

But even though now part of her still held her breath, bracing herself for things to go wrong, they didn't. Instead, amazingly, things just kept improving. Each day that dawned somehow seemed to be even better than the last.

There were evenings when she was secretly afraid to go to sleep, fearing that when she woke up in the morning, she would find that it had all been just a dream. A wonderful, wonderful dream that, like all dreams, had come to an end.

But it didn't end.

It continued. Continued being gratifyingly magnificent.

Connor worked on the ranch with Cole during the day, and at night, he would come home to her and Jamie. Home to do wonderfully normal, simple things. They'd have dinner, he'd play with the baby and then, after

Jamie would fall asleep and Rita would retreat to her room, they would have their time together.

And every night, when they made love, it was as if it was a brand-new, exciting event. They discovered things about one another, about pleasuring one another, that made it all amazingly fresh for her.

Amy felt incredibly lucky and happier than she had ever been in her entire life.

The best part of it for her was that they were becoming a family—a real family. Amy couldn't have been more thrilled about that, finding she and Jamie easily melded into the fold that comprised the McCullough clan. There was a sense of contentment in knowing she was not only accepted by Connor, she had been accepted by his whole family.

"Family life suits you," Cody commented that Sunday afternoon as he, Cole and Cassidy's husband, Will, sat in the living room after dinner was over, watching the gaggle of kids who made up the McCulloughs' younger generation, while Amy, Cassidy, Devon and Stacy helped Rita clear the table and deal with the dirty dishes as well as the pots and pans.

"Not exactly a news flash," Connor said as he picked up Jamie to quiet him because the boy was fussing. "Family life has always suited me."

"What Cody is trying to say in his own ineloquent way," Will explained, flashing a grin at his oldest brother-in-law, "is your *own* family life."

"Yeah," Cole agreed, adding his voice to the discussion. "Up until now, when you said 'family' that just meant you hanging out with us and our individual families." He looked affectionately at his twins, who appeared to be engaged in some sort of a race, crawling toward the kitchen. He was quick to get in their way, thereby calling an end to it. "Ever since Amy got here with her son, things have changed."

Connor snorted, waving a dismissive hand at the other men. "You guys have been drinking too much holiday cheer," he told them. "You're all hallucinating."

"No, we're not," Will insisted. He'd been friends with all of them for a lot of years now and had been practically like a brother years before he had married into the family. "What we are is really glad for you."

"Yeah," Cole chimed in, herding his twins back toward the communal playpen in the center of the living room. "You deserve to be happy."

"Not to mention just as sleepless as the rest of us," Cody said, putting his daughter on his knee and bouncing her to entertain the toddler.

"Desserts are on the table," Cassidy announced as she stood in the doorway, calling them back to the dining room. "Better get a move on and come back to the table before Rita gets insulted."

"Wouldn't want that," Will agreed, sweeping his son into his arms in one smooth movement, bringing him along with him.

The others followed suit, picking up the babies—in Cole's case, two of them—and heading toward the dining room.

As he carried Jamie and followed the others into the next room, Connor looked around. His brothers were right. He did feel different somehow. Happier. He felt as if he had his own family now and he intended to do everything in his power to keep it that way.

When the time was right, he was going to ask Amy to marry him.

*Privately*, he silently stressed. Although he loved his siblings and was close to them, he felt that a proposal wasn't meant to be a three-ring event. He wanted Amy all to himself when he finally asked her that all-important question.

At least, that was his plan.

CHRISTMAS WAS QUICKLY approaching and she was getting involved in planning the family meal with Rita. Amy was so excited and happy she felt she was going to burst.

In her estimation, everything was just getting more and more perfect, she thought late one evening as she lay in Connor's arms.

But even with all this happiness around her, she was aware of one possible fly in the ointment.

A "fly" that could ruin everything.

"You're frowning," Connor noted as he looked down and saw the expression on her face.

"Am I?" she asked, her eyes widening innocently.

She could tell that she wasn't fooling Connor. She really needed to work on maintaining a poker face. Every thought she had seemed to imprint itself on her face.

Crooking his finger under her chin, Connor tilted her head up until their eyes met.

"Yes, you are," he told her. "Has my performance rating gone down?" he teased. "Because if it has, I can do better." Running his hand slowly along the soft curves of her body, he began to show her.

Anticipation shimmered through her veins, raising her body temperature. "If you were any better, you'd be in the Smithsonian, preserved under glass to keep you safe from other women."

He laughed. "You're the only woman I'm interested in," he told her. He pressed a kiss to her shoulder before growing serious. "But that still doesn't explain why you're frowning."

Amy debated saying that he was imagining things, that she wasn't frowning, just thinking. But she didn't want to lie to Connor, not even a little white lie. She wanted him to feel that she had always been honest with him.

So, at the risk of shattering what had been, up until now, a beautiful evening, she told him the truth, confessing what was bothering her, what she couldn't seem to bury or simply forget about.

"There's been no word from Clay."

Connor raised himself up on his elbow, silently studying her for a long moment before asking, "Do you *want* to hear from Clay?"

"Oh no," she cried. "Not personally," she said quickly, trying to make herself clear. "I meant that he hasn't responded to Cash about the divorce papers. He hasn't signed them and sent them back."

"No, he hasn't," Connor acknowledged.

Though he hadn't said anything about the matter to her, he was keenly aware of the fact that Clay Patton hadn't gotten in contact with Amy's lawyer, either to send back the signed divorce documents, or even to rail and make his own demands. He'd already called Cash a number of times to see if there had been any word from Amy's no-account soon-to-be ex and been disappointed to hear that there hadn't been.

"But look at the bright side. Even if he doesn't sign the papers, Cash said that you can still get the divorce," he reminded her, continuing to run his fingers lovingly along her body. "It'll just be a divorce by default. One way or the other, you are going to shed that no-good cowboy and be a free woman," he told her. "Very, very soon. Now, no more talk about Clay." He moved her and drew her body over his. "We've got more important subjects demanding our attention."

"Oh?" she asked brightly, feigning ignorance. "Such as?"

"Such as which side of your neck I should nibble on next," Connor said. "This side?" He chose the side closest to him, pressing his lips against it. He heard her catch her breath and it fed his own excitement. "Or this side?" he asked, shifting her so that he could kiss the other side of her neck, as well.

"You know," he told her, fitting her torso against his own, "I really can't decide." His lips were barely a fraction away from her skin. His breath sent hot shock waves all through her body. "Which is your favorite side?" he asked, his warm breath caressing her.

She felt his lips curving in a smile against her skin. She couldn't help moving against him in growing anticipation of what was to come.

"I can't decide, either," she breathed, struggling to be coherent. "Do it again."

"With pleasure," he said just before he began kissing the sides of her neck again.

BUT AMY'S CONCERN regarding the divorce papers continued to linger, surfacing the next day after Connor had gone out to do his daily chores and tend to the horses. She knew that until the divorce was a done deal and became a thing of the past, it would go on haunting her. Part of her was still afraid that Clay would storm back into her life, not because he wanted her, not because he wanted to reconcile and make an attempt at a fresh start, but because, as she had told Connor, she had left him and his pride would not stand for something like that.

Maybe she was making too big a deal of it, Amy thought, trying to comfort herself. Maybe Clay was as glad to be rid of her as she was to be rid of him.

Maybe.

But in her heart, she doubted it.

Knowing that focusing on this would only drive her crazy, Amy forced herself to think about all the good things that were in her life. Good things like Jamie, who seemed to be thriving now that they were away from Clay's toxic behavior. Good things like looking forward to spending Christmas with Connor and his big family.

And, best of all, for the first time in her life, she was with someone she loved who behaved as if he loved her back. Someone who made her look forward to each day—and especially to each night.

Even if nothing ever changed, she would be happy to stay right here like this for the rest of her life.

"What would you say," Connor asked her at the table

a few mornings later, "if, right after breakfast, we take a trip into town?"

She knew how Connor felt about faithfully following his daily routine. She didn't want him changing things because of her. "What about the ranch?"

"The ranch'll stay here," he answered, a mischievous grin curving his mouth.

Amy gave him a look. "You know what I mean. Don't you have work to do?"

The key to a happy life, he had come to believe, was balance.

"Yes, but I can work twice as hard tomorrow," he told her. "I think you need an outing and I need to get a little shopping done."

She didn't understand why he needed to go to the general store. For the most part, it was something he shied away from if he could help it. "I thought Rita already got supplies this week," she pointed out.

"Maybe I'm not shopping for supplies," he replied, trying his best not to grin. "Maybe I need to do some Christmas shopping."

Amy laughed in response.

He looked at her, puzzled. "What's so funny?"

She waved her hand, as if silently asking for his indulgence. "I'm sorry. I just can't picture you going Christmas shopping."

"I'll have you know that there are a lot of things you don't know about me," he said, pretending to be mysterious.

Her eyes sparkled as she answered, "Apparently.

Okay, I'll get ready right after breakfast. I've already fed Jamie."

Connor nodded. "Well, that'll make it easier for Rita."

She wasn't sure she understood what he meant by that. "Easier?"

"She'll have less to do," he explained. "I thought we'd have her watch Jamie while we go into town. We're not going to be gone all that long and I'd like this outing to be just the two of us—unless that doesn't meet with your approval."

He was always being so considerate of her feelings, she thought. It never ceased to surprise her, especially after the way she had been treated before. Connor almost seemed too good to be true. Every day in every way, the man just kept winning her heart all over again, Amy thought.

"It meets with my wholehearted approval," she told him.

That was the answer he was hoping for. "Good. Then I'll go tell Rita that she gets to enjoy Jamie for a few hours and you go get ready."

She was gone like a flash, leaving him standing there, chuckling under his breath. Amy never ceased to delight him, Connor thought in utter amazement.

His main reason for going into town was to see if he could coax her into pointing out something that she'd like for Christmas. He had a feeling that her five previous Christmases had been the kind that would have gladdened the heart of a Scrooge prior to his reformation, and he wanted this, their first Christmas together, to be a special one for her.

And while they were in town, he also wanted to quickly swing by the law firm for a face-to-face meeting with Cash. He wanted to find out firsthand if there had been any word back from Clay. He highly doubted it, confident that at the very least Cash would have given either Amy or him a call if there had been any feedback. However, since he was going to be in town, it didn't hurt to ask.

More than anything, he wanted to set Amy's mind at ease and he knew that wasn't going to be the case until this whole matter was over and behind her.

She wouldn't have to be going through this if he had only had the courage of his convictions and asked her to marry him the way he'd wanted to five years ago. If he had, he would have spared her all the anguish she had gone through.

But by the same token, he reminded himself, she wouldn't have had Jamie, and anyone could see that Jamie meant the world to her.

*Every dark cloud has a silver lining*, his father had been fond of saying.

Probably because there had been so many dark clouds in their world at the time. But despite all that, despite the death of his wife and all the rough times they'd had, his father, the man he had always admired the most in this world, had never given up.

*If you're going through hell, just keep on going* had been one of his father's mottoes, and that was exactly what he intended to do. He intended to keep on going no matter what. Keep on going until he managed to get that divorce for Amy, come hell or high water.

And once that was in place—which he really hoped was soon—he intended to ask her to marry him. Because even after the short amount of time they'd had together, he could not begin to imagine life without Amy—or without her son.

Cody was right. They were a family now. Somehow, when he wasn't looking, all the pieces had come together. Those pieces that had always, until recently, felt missing from his life—they had come together. And now he felt whole because they were a family, he and Amy and Jamie. And nothing had ever felt so right to him before.

He intended to fight to keep this family. And that meant sweeping Clay Patton out of Amy's life once and for all.

Connor couldn't wait to make that happen.

## Chapter Eighteen

The first thing Amy noticed as they drove into Forever was that the town Christmas tree was now fully decked out. All the boxes and ladders that had been part of the decorating ceremony had been cleaned up and put away, allowing attention to be focused on the finished product in all its glory.

"The tree looks absolutely beautiful," Amy noted in awe.

Wanting to get a better, unobstructed view of the tree, she rolled down the truck window on her side so she could stick out her head.

Cold air came in, but it didn't have any impact for a couple of minutes. She was that enthralled with what she could see. It took a couple of minutes before the nippy air got the better of her and she rolled the window up.

Sitting back in her seat, she was almost glowing as she looked at Connor. "You were right."

"About?"

"That knowing I was part of helping to make that all come about by decorating the tree *does* feel good." She

sighed as she recalled other Christmases from her ado-
lescence. "I missed that feeling these last five years."

"Don't think about that part," he told her. "Just think
about the fact that you're here now and part of Forever
again."

She saw the diner on their left. "Are we going to be
stopping at the diner?"

Aside from seeing Cash and visiting the general store,
Connor was open to anything she was up for. "If you
want to."

She nodded. Unlike her first trip into town, she was
through with hiding.

"I want to. But business first, then pleasure," she said.
"Let's go talk to Cash." She saw the surprised expression on Connor's face and almost laughed. "What, you
didn't think I knew that was why you wanted to come
into Forever?"

He didn't want it to seem as if he was trying to put
one over on her. "I thought that since we were going to
be in town anyway—"

"Uh-huh," she murmured.

She knew his heart was in the right place, and since
she'd voiced her concern about Clay not signing the divorce papers, this was his way of trying to restore her
peace of mind. Connor was really one of a kind, she
thought, and she had no idea why she hadn't seen that
years earlier.

"C'mon," she urged, eager to get talking to the lawyer out of the way. "Let's do this so we can enjoy the
rest of our visit."

Cash looked up, surprised to see them when Cassidy ushered her brother and Amy into his office. Saving the file he'd been reviewing on his computer screen, Cash half rose in his chair.

"Connor, Amy, please, sit down," he said, gesturing toward the two chairs that were right in front of his desk. His brow furrowed slightly as he tried to remember. "Did I forget an appointment today?"

"No, we didn't make one," Connor confessed. "We're not here to take up any of your time," he explained as both he and Amy remained standing. They intended to leave as soon as this was out of the way. "We just wanted to ask if you'd heard anything back from—"

"Clay Patton?" Cash guessed. "No, regrettably, I haven't. I would have notified you immediately, Amy," he assured her.

Amy nodded, flashing an apologetic smile at the man. "That's what we thought. It's just that I was hoping maybe you'd gotten caught up in something and didn't get a chance to call me."

Cash grinned. "Amy, you haven't been gone *that* long," he pointed out. "This is Forever. Not exactly a hotbed of illegal shenanigans. All I've been dealing with are just the regular wills and an occasional property-line dispute." He decided to fill her in on the steps he'd taken regarding her case. "I sent a courier to serve Clay with the divorce papers, which he did. So if Clay wasn't aware of your intentions to divorce him before, he definitely is now."

"And there's been no word?" Amy confirmed, disappointed.

"Other than the barrage of curses Clay heaped on the courier? I'm afraid not. We'll give him to the end of the month," Cash went on to say, "and if he makes no effort to get in contact with my office or mail back the divorce papers, we'll go ahead and start the process to have you divorce him in absentia." The look in his eyes was nothing if not encouraging. "Hang in there, Amy," he told her. "This'll all be over with soon."

Amy sighed deeply. "Not soon enough for me," she said with sincerity.

Connor took hold of her arm, tugging lightly and drawing her attention toward the door.

"C'mon," he encouraged. "Let's go get some of Miss Joan's pie. Everything always looks better after some of her pie."

"Amen to that," Cash agreed. "Tell my stepgrandmother I said hi. And the minute I know anything, so will you."

Amy smiled her gratitude. "Can't ask for more than that."

"It's going to be all right," Connor said with wholehearted sincerity the moment they were outside the law firm.

She wasn't nearly as sure as he seemed to be about the matter. "Clay probably tore up the papers and threw them out."

"Doesn't matter," Connor said, then reminded her, "Remember what Cash said. You don't need Clay's okay to go ahead with this. It'll take a bit longer," he granted, "but ultimately you'll get the results you want—to be free of him."

She took a deep breath, trying to remain positive. "You're right."

"Not always," Connor admitted. "But in this case," he said with confidence, "I am."

She slipped her arm through his. He was such a positive person. Connor was good for her. "Let's walk to Miss Joan's."

"You sure?" he asked uncertainly. "It's kind of cold out."

"It's crisp," she corrected. "Crisp and clear. And right now, I feel like walking."

He smiled at her, willing to do anything she wanted to do. All he ever wanted was to make her happy. "Then we'll walk."

Amy was very tempted to tell him that he was spoiling her, but she was afraid he might take it as a criticism and she was enjoying being indulged way too much to have it stop abruptly. So she said nothing. She merely looked up at Connor and smiled her gratitude.

ALTHOUGH SHE WAS all the way across the diner, Miss Joan spotted them the moment they walked in. She withheld a greeting, waiting to see where they'd sit. When they approached the counter, she was obviously pleased. There was even a hint of a smile on her thin lips as she made her way over to them.

"Haven't seen you two in a while," she commented.

"It hasn't been that long," Connor told her.

Miss Joan pinned him with a look. "When you get to be my age, every day is long. So, what'll it be?" she asked.

"We'll have two coffees and some of your smile-inducing pie," Connor said.

"Angel's pie. Angel makes the pie," she informed them as if they didn't know. "I make the coffee."

Connor smiled. Miss Joan was almost fanatical when it came to not taking credit when it wasn't hers to take. Inclining his head, he corrected himself. "Then we'll have two cups of your coffee and two slices of Angel's pie."

"For here?" Miss Joan asked, her eyes washing over them. "Or to go?"

"For here," Connor answered.

Miss Joan nodded her approval. "Good," the woman pronounced. "Be back in a minute," she promised, making eye contact with Amy rather than Connor. It was as if she was telling the young woman that there was a covenant between them.

True to her word, Miss Joan returned with the slices of pie in less than a minute. The coffee took her another minute to pour and bring over.

She placed the small metal container filled with cream between them. "Anything else?"

Amy smiled her thanks. "Not right now."

Miss Joan nodded as if in response to some private conversation she'd been having in her head. "Then I'll let you enjoy Angel's pie in peace," she told them, withdrawing.

"Well, that's a first," Connor commented under his breath.

Despite his quiet voice, Miss Joan responded, "I heard that," from further down the counter.

Connor grinned in response. "I knew you would." Like everyone else in town, he was aware that there was nothing wrong with either the woman's hearing or her vision, despite the fact that Miss Joan would never see middle age again.

"I feel sinful, having dessert without having a meal first," Amy confessed to him, sinking her fork into the pie on her plate again. "But this is just too good to pass up."

Affection filled him the way it did nearly a dozen times a day. Every time he looked at her, he couldn't believe that she was back in his life, that he'd been granted a second chance at happiness.

"This isn't even *close* to sinful," Connor said. "But if you're feeling guilty, we can stick around and have lunch later if you'd like."

She did, but there was a slight problem. "What about Rita? We told her we'd only be gone for a couple of hours at most."

"I know, but Jamie's only six months old—"

"Almost seven," Amy interjected proudly.

"Only almost seven months old," he amended without skipping a beat. "It's not as if she has to chase after him all over the house. Rita might look formidable, but that woman really *enjoys* taking care of babies, so I know she won't mind if we're gone a few more hours than we said we would be."

Amy looked down at her plate and saw that she'd finished the pie without even realizing it.

It had gone down far too easily, she mused. "Why

don't we do that shopping you wanted to do and then we'll see?" she suggested.

"Sounds good," Connor answered. Looking around the diner for Miss Joan, he raised his hand to get her attention.

"Something else?" the woman asked as she walked over to them.

"Just the check for now," Connor told her.

Taking out the pad she always kept in the pocket of her uniform, Miss Joan quickly wrote down a total, tore off the page and pressed it into his hand.

Glancing at it, he thought that it seemed to be lower than he'd expected.

"You sure about this?" he asked her.

"Don't ever question me in my own place, boy," Miss Joan warned him. "Of course I'm sure. Now take that over to Nina and be on your way," she instructed, nodding at the cashier.

He wasn't about to argue with her. But Connor shook his head as he crossed to the cashier.

"Don't know how that woman makes any money," he said to Amy.

"I don't think she's in it for the money," Amy said.

He gave the cashier more than what was on the receipt. When she began to give him change, he shook his head.

"Keep it," he told the girl. Turning to Amy, he replied to her observation. "You're probably right. The diner is a way of life for her."

"That really was very good," Amy said, commenting on the pie as they walked out of the diner.

"Yeah, it was." The wind had picked up, almost swirling around them. It felt colder than it had when they'd walked over from the law office. "Why don't you go back inside and wait for me while I go get the truck?" he suggested.

But Amy shook her head, turning down his offer. "I'm not that frail, Connor," she assured him. "And I'm not about to turn into an icicle if I walk to the general store with you."

Connor turned up his collar. "Just remember I offered," he told her as he held out his elbow to her again.

Smiling warmly, Amy slipped her arm through it. "Don't worry—I'm not going to sue you if I get pneumonia." And then she laughed when she saw the concerned look come over his face. "I'm just kidding, Connor. Really. I'm *not* cold."

He still had his doubts about the wisdom of this. He didn't think she was dressed warm enough for this kind of weather. He'd been so glad to get her out of the house, he hadn't really paid attention to what she'd put on.

"It *is* cold," he pointed out.

Amy shrugged in response. "Is it? I don't feel a thing." She wrapped her other arm around the one she'd already linked with, hugging him. "As a matter of fact, I feel all warm and toasty inside," she said, looking up at him as they walked in approximately the direction of the general store.

"Well now, isn't that just too sweet for words?"

Amy froze.

She would have recognized that sarcastic, belittling voice anywhere. The next moment, as she turned around to face the man who'd made her life so miserable, she felt Connor's arm slip protectively around her shoulders.

Clay Patton's dark eyes were regarding her with contempt. She met his stare head-on, no longer afraid, no longer ready to turn and run. He was still as tall and darkly handsome with thick, almost black hair as he had been when she'd first fallen in love with him, but she now saw Clay as a little, little man. She wondered how she could have been so blind and foolish to not see him for what he really was.

"Didn't take you long to find yourself a sucker, did it, Amy?" Clay asked, sneering. "What did you do, play the pathetic, wounded little sparrow so that he'd feel sorry for you?"

For the first time, Amy saw anger crease Connor's face.

"The only thing you need to do," Connor informed the man before him, "is take yourself over to Cash Taylor's law office and give him those divorce papers you were sent—signed."

"Oh no," Clay said nastily, "I'm not making it that easy for you, McCullough. You want my wife, you're going to have to pay for her. *Dearly*," he underscored. "You understand my meaning?"

"You always were a piece of worthless filth, Patton," Connor told him. "You don't deserve someone like Amy. You never did. And she's not your property. She never was. Nobody's going to be paying you for anything."

All the anger he'd felt toward the man when he'd pieced together things that Amy had suffered at Clay's hands was now bubbling up to the surface, threatening to spill over. He struggled to hold himself in check.

The sneer on Clay's lips deepened, transforming his sculpted features into a mask of ugliness. "You don't and you'll be sorry," Clay threatened.

"No," Connor said, sounding far more calm than he actually felt. "You even *try* anything and you'll be the one who's sorry. Lift one finger against Amy and I'll get your hide thrown into jail so fast, it'll make your head spin so hard, you'll be throwing up.

"Now I know you're not exactly the brightest penny in the drawer, but get this through your thick skull. Nobody's on your side, Clay. Everyone's on Amy's. So for once in your life, do the decent thing. Sign those papers and then go back down the hole you slithered out of and get out of her life."

Fury blazed in Clay's eyes as he glared at Amy. "Is that what you want?" Clay demanded, almost shrieking. "You're picking Dudley Do-Right over here over me?"

She saw that Connor was about to place himself between Clay and her again, but she put her hand on his arm, silently stopping him. She needed to handle this herself if she was *ever* going to hold her head up high.

"Well?" Clay demanded, apparently taking the fact that she had stopped Connor from doing anything to mean that he had won.

"You're damn straight I am," she said fiercely. "I'd pick Connor seven ways from Sunday over you because he's ten times the man you *ever* were. He doesn't have to pump up his ego by finding ways to belittle me."

Enraged, Clay made a grab for her. Reacting quickly,

Connor punched him, sending him reeling backward and falling to the ground. Clay scrambled to his feet, cursing at both Connor and Amy. Snarling, he was about to tackle Connor when they heard the unmistakable sound of a gun being cocked.

"Hold it right there and take a step back, Patton, if you know what's good for you," Sheriff Rick Santiago ordered the man in a voice that was deceptively calm.

# Chapter Nineteen

"You saw it, Sheriff," Clay shouted, so livid that his face was turning red. "You saw what McCullough did! He attacked me! That maniac hit me first!"

Beside himself with fury, Patton appeared to be all but foaming at the mouth. It was at that moment that it seemed to dawn on him there was a crowd gathering around him and McCullough—and he hated looking like a fool.

Drawn by the sound of the angry, raised voices, a dozen customers and employees had filed out of the general store while at least a dozen more had glimpsed the goings-on through the diner windows and had come out to see what was happening.

"We all saw it, Patton," Rick answered, nodding at the people around them. "And the way *I* saw it, Connor was just trying to protect Amy."

"Protect Amy?" Patton jeered. "She's *my* wife. I've got rights, damn it!" he shouted, the veins popping out along his neck. "I've got a right to take back what's mine. Amy's my wife and I've got a right to—"

"No, she *was* your wife," Connor emphasized, unable to just stand by and listen to the man's rantings a second longer.

Anyone looking at Connor's face could see that the rancher was doing a very slow, very steady burn and it was just a matter of time before he would lose his cool and erupt.

"You were officially notified, Clay," Amy said, stepping in to face up to her former husband. There was disdain in her eyes as she told the man, "I'm divorcing you."

"No, you're not!" Clay bellowed. "I'm not signing the papers!"

"For your information, you don't have to," Amy countered, her voice as tranquil and quiet as his was irate and loud. "I've got more than enough grounds and I will get that divorce whether you sign those papers or not."

"I don't know what kind of a game you and your boyfriend here are playing, but if this is a shakedown, you're not getting a penny out of me!" Clay's voice had risen so high, he was all but screeching.

Her eyes were an icy blue as she looked at the man who had made her life so miserable over the last five years. "I don't want anything from you except to never have to lay eyes on you again."

Rick glanced briefly in Connor's direction before he turned his attention to Patton. It was obvious that he didn't take kindly to anyone disrupting the peace in his town. Rick rested his hand on the hilt of the weapon he had just holstered, his meaning quite clear.

"I'd listen to Ms. Donavan," Rick said, deliberately using Amy's maiden name, "if I were you. In my opinion, I'd say that you were getting off pretty easy."

Patton glared at Amy. "You're going to be sorry, you bitch," he warned her. Connor took a step forward, ready to pummel Patton for insulting her, but Amy had her hand on his shoulder, stopping him. Patton shrank back a little, but he couldn't resist one last threat. "And when you are, don't come crawling back to me."

"Do me a favor, Clay," Amy said, raising her voice so he could hear her over the growing din as Patton opened the door on the driver's side of his blazing red sports car.

"What?" he spit.

"Hold your breath," Amy answered sweetly.

Shouting several more curses at her from the safety of his car, Patton slammed the door and locked it before Connor could reach him to make him eat his words.

She could tell that Connor looked ready to yank her former husband out of the car, undoubtedly to make him apologize.

Hand on the car's door, Connor appeared ready to rip it off its hinges. Behind the door's rolled-up window, Clay seemed properly terrified.

"Don't," Amy pleaded, holding on to Connor's arm even though she knew there was no way she could stop him if he did decide to pull Clay out of the car. "He's not worth it and you don't want to give him the satisfaction of stooping to his level."

And then, both because she wanted to and because she knew that Clay was still watching, Amy threw her arms around Connor's neck, raised herself up on her toes and kissed him. Kissed him as if he was a soldier coming home from the war and she hadn't seen him in over five long years.

It took very little for Amy to get lost in that kiss. And even less to forget that Patton was watching them—and fuming.

She was vaguely aware that the crowd that had gathered to see what all the commotion was about was now actively cheering them on. She also heard the very distinct sound of Clay's sports car, revving up and then peeling out of Forever.

Drawing back, Connor kept his hands wrapped around her waist. "Was that to show up Patton?" he asked.

"No," she answered honestly, smiling up at the man she credited for having saved her, emotionally and literally. "That was for me. And to say thank you."

"Okay, everybody," Rick announced, turning toward the crowd and addressing them. "Show's over. Go back to whatever you were all doing."

"Not much of anything, Sheriff," Harlan, one of Miss Joan's steadiest customers, said, referring to what had occupied at least the people in the diner. "And this—" he indicated Amy and Connor with his gnarled finger "—was a whole lot more interesting than sittin' on a stool, having lunch."

Another one of Miss Joan's patrons, Ben Crawford, gave Amy a fatherly pat on the shoulder.

"Don't you worry. That no-account's probably gone for good. He's too much of a coward not to be. No offense," he said as an aside to Amy.

"None taken," she assured the man.

"But just in case," Ben went on, looking over his shoulder at his friends, "we'll all keep a lookout for him, won't we, boys?" A chorus of murmurs agreed. Dutifully, Ben looked over toward Rick. "And not to worry, Sheriff. We'll come straight to you if we see him."

"You'd better," Rick told the man, his gaze sweeping over all the people who were in the crowd. "All of you," he added for good measure. "Now move along. No sense in blocking the street—unless it's to look up at that big Christmas tree."

The crowd obediently broke up. Taking Amy's hand, Connor led her away from the point of confrontation, as well.

"Not exactly the way I intended today to go," Connor said, frowning. "Are you all right, Amy?"

Walking beside Connor, she didn't hesitate with her answer. "I got to finally tell that walking narcissist what I thought of him and then I got to kiss my guy." Her eyes were shining. "I'm terrific."

"Yes," he agreed warmly with a grin, "you are."

And then Amy replayed the words she'd used in her head, afraid that maybe she had scared him off by assuming too much and telling him so.

"Um, Connor, when I called you 'my guy,' I didn't mean…"

"What, that you thought of me as your guy?" he asked. "Am I being demoted? Because if I am, that kind of puts a kink in my plans."

"Demoted?" she repeated. Stunned, she looked at him. "You mean that you *want* to be my guy?"

She knew the term sounded a little juvenile, but right now, she felt as if she was eighteen all over again. Eighteen and this time finally headed in the right direction.

"Wait," she cried as the rest of what he'd just said

replayed itself in her head. "What kink?" she asked. "What plans?"

"Oh, so *now* you're interested?" Connor asked, feigning surprise.

She stopped walking. She didn't want to play it safe anymore, didn't want to keep herself and her feelings under wraps anymore. *No risk, no gain*, she told herself, and she really, really wanted to be able to gain the happiness that was shimmering right before her eyes. What she and Connor had had these last few days was something she had aspired to all her life, and now that she'd had a taste of it, she knew she would never want to go back to the way her life had been.

"I have always been interested," she admitted seriously. "I was just too dumb to realize it."

"Hey, don't run yourself down," he said. "If I hadn't kept coming up with excuses why I couldn't step up and tell you how I felt about you, things might have gone a whole different way right from the start. But I didn't and that's on me.

"We can't change any of the past, Amy. We can only learn from our mistakes and move on. And what I want to do," he told her, his voice growing lower, "is move on with you."

"*With* me, not *from* me, right?" she asked, wanting to be absolutely sure.

"With you," he repeated with feeling. "Come back to the truck with me."

She thought he was saying that so he could shelter her from the wind that was still picking up. "I said I wasn't cold."

"This has nothing to do with the weather or you being cold," Connor said. "Just come back to the truck."

He sounded so serious, she wasn't about to argue with him. "Okay."

Amy assumed the scene with Clay had put a damper on the rest of the day for him and Connor just wanted to go back to the ranch. She certainly couldn't blame him, so she didn't try to talk him out of it, or mention the fact that he hadn't done the shopping he'd said he wanted to do.

Reaching the truck they'd left parked near the law firm, she got in, put her seat belt on and waited for Connor to start the engine.

But he didn't. And he didn't put his seat belt on. He just sat there, being very quiet.

Too quiet, Amy thought.

"Um, Connor, the truck won't go on its own. You have to put the key in," she prodded, hoping a little humor would make him come around. She couldn't help wondering what was going on in his mind.

Had that scene with Clay ruined more than just their outing? Was the confrontation and what was said making Connor rethink everything? Especially their budding relationship?

When he still didn't say anything, Amy grew nervous. She didn't want to lose him.

"Connor? Talk to me."

With a slight nod, Connor began talking very quietly. "I was going to wait until all the i's were dotted and the t's were crossed."

He might be talking, but she was *not* understanding what he was talking about.

"Wait for what?" she asked, growing steadily more nervous. "What i's, what t's?"

Connor realized that he was getting ahead of himself—and losing her in the process. He tried again. "Your divorce. I was going to wait until that was resolved and you had it behind you."

It still wasn't making any sense to her. "You still haven't told me. Wait for what?"

Connor felt as if he was tripping over his own tongue, but in his defense, he'd never done this before. "I was going to wait until all this was cleared up and you didn't feel like it was hanging over your head."

He *still* wasn't answering her question.

"Wait for *what*? Why were you waiting?" she cried, enunciating every word. "And why are you telling me this in your truck? Why aren't we going to the general store to go Christmas shopping the way you said you wanted to?"

She would have felt safer if they were outside. Connor wouldn't risk making her cry if there were people around, she thought. He was too much of a gentleman for that.

But she was still worried she wasn't going to like what was coming.

"We're in my truck instead of the general store because I wanted to keep this private, at least for the first five minutes," he qualified, his lips quirking in a half smile. "And I wanted to do this now because, despite all my good reasons to the contrary, I don't want to wait any longer."

He was pausing again, she thought, thoroughly frustrated and fighting the urge to go running down his throat in order to pull the words out.

"Wait any longer for *what*, Connor?" she said, fisting her hands in her lap.

Rather than answer her, Connor leaned slightly over to one side so he could dig something out of his front pocket. Something he'd been carrying around since they'd left the ranch this morning.

"Connor, what is it?" she demanded, feeling more tightly wound up than a spring that was about to go shooting off at the smallest touch.

Before answering Amy, Connor drew his hand out of his pocket and opened it. His fingers had been closed around a small, lovingly polished diamond ring.

"This was my mother's. My dad gave it to her the night he proposed to her. He'd saved up for a whole year to buy it," Connor explained, adding, "I know that they'd both want you to have this." He took a breath, trying to steady his nerves. "Amy Donavan, I've been in love with you for a very long, long time. Will you marry me?" he asked, his voice deliberately low to keep it from cracking. "I know this is sudden and you don't have to give me your answer right away—"

He'd barely finished his sentence before she'd grabbed the heart-shaped engagement ring and slipped it on her trembling finger.

It fit.

She felt that was a good omen.

Throwing her arms around Connor's neck, she cried, "Yes!" just before she sealed her mouth to his, kissing him with all the emotion that had suddenly welled up within her.

When she finally drew her lips away, although her arms remained around his neck, he looked at her, equally stunned and pleased at the same time.

"Are you sure?" he asked, not wanting her to get carried away because of what had happened earlier.

"I could kiss you again to show you how sure I am," she offered.

"I'd like that," he said.

The smile on her lips began in her eyes, lighting all of her up.

"Yeah, me, too," she told him right before she went on to show him just how much.

## *Epilogue*

It was Christmas Day and the entire family was gathered at the house, the way they always were to celebrate the holiday.

Because of all the noise, Amy, who had Jamie on her lap, shook her head and pointed to her ear, indicating that she hadn't heard what he'd just said.

Moving closer, Connor sat down on the sofa next to her, leaned in and whispered the words into her ear. "You're beaming, you know."

Her eyes instantly crinkled at the corners as she smiled at him. "I know. I can't help it. This is the most wonderful Christmas I've had in a very long time. Maybe ever," she said.

"But you've been awake since the crack of dawn and you worked nonstop all morning and half the afternoon," he pointed out as he slipped his arm around her and drew her closer to him.

"That's part of what makes all this wonderful," she answered. Right now, she felt so happy, she thought she was going to burst. "I was helping get everything ready. Rita even let me help her cook dinner." Which, in her eyes, was a big deal. "Besides—" she put her hand on his chest, loving the way she could feel his heart beat beneath her palm "—I didn't get started working until almost eight."

His smile was for her alone, despite the fact that the rest of his family was there with them in the living room, enjoying the gifts that had been exchanged and opened, but most of all, just enjoying being together as a family.

"I thought maybe you'd enjoy starting a new Christmas tradition," Connor told her with a sexy wink, referring to the way they had started the morning.

"Oh, was that what that was?" she asked, amusement curving her mouth as she recalled their lovemaking.

"Uh-huh."

"Hey, you two, save that for later," Cody called out, sitting on the floor next to the Christmas tree as he played with his daughter. "This is a G-rated family gathering."

"Said the old married man," Connor teased.

"Hold it down, people. It's so noisy in here, I can't even hear myself think," Cole told the others, raising his voice.

"You? I didn't know you *could* think," Connor shot back.

"Just for that, I'll tell him I couldn't find you," Cole replied, pretending to turn away.

That got Connor's attention and he got up off the sofa, approaching his brother. "Tell who you couldn't find me?"

In response, Cole held up the receiver to the landline that Connor continued to maintain. His grandfather had been the first to have it installed and Connor was rather sentimental about keeping the old landline even though they all owned cell phones now.

He crossed over to Cole. "Who's on the line?" he asked.

"Why don't you find out for yourself?" Cole suggested, holding the receiver out to him. The grin on his face was wide enough to make the Cheshire cat envious.

Taking the phone out of Cole's hand, Connor said, "Hello, this is Connor McCullough."

"Connor, this is Cash Taylor. I didn't want to bother you in case you were just about to start having dinner with your family."

"No, we're all done. We get started early around here because of the kids' bedtimes," Connor explained. "So, what's up?"

Curious and concerned that it might be bad news because of the timing of the call, Amy had crossed over to offer Connor her silent support if he needed it.

"I thought you'd want to hear this right away. It seems that confrontation in the middle of the town square left Clay Patton with a bad taste in his mouth. One he wanted to get rid of and forget as fast as possible."

"Hey, hold it down, everyone," Cassidy ordered as the noise in the room began to increase again. She'd been watching the expression on her brother's face. "Connor needs to hear this."

"Cash, what are you saying?" Connor asked the man on the other end of the line, trying not to let his imagination run away with him.

"Patton stormed into my house a few minutes ago.

Seems the man doesn't realize it's Christmas. Anyway, he slapped the divorce papers into my hand, then stomped out," Cash told him.

"Were they signed?" Connor asked, afraid to take anything for granted.

"They were signed," Cash answered. "Merry Christmas, Connor."

"And the same to you, Cash," Connor replied, feeling a little dazed as he hung up the phone.

Amy handed Jamie over to Cassidy and went up to Connor. "Well?" she cried, anxiously hoping that Connor would say the words she was praying to hear.

He turned from the wall phone and then caught her up in his arms and spun her around.

"You are officially a free woman, Amy Donavan," he told her. Setting her down again, Connor said, "We can get married now."

Stunned, thrilled, Amy did her best to try to put on a serious face as she said, "Well, I don't want to rush into anything."

"What?" He didn't know if she was serious or pulling his leg.

"Oh, come here, you idiot," she cried, throwing her arms around his neck. "I told you this was the best Christmas ever!"

"And the best," he promised her just before he kissed her, "is yet to be."

"I am going to hold you to that, Connor McCullough," she told him breathlessly.

His smile scrambled her pulse as he said, "I'm counting on it."

As he brought his mouth down to hers, he heard the rest of his family, even Rita, applauding them and cheering.

And no one was cheering more than he was… He was just doing it internally.

\* \* \* \* \*

# Get 2 Free Books,

## HARLEQUIN® Western Romance

## Plus 2 Free Gifts—

### just for trying the Reader Service!

# Western Romance

*Rodeo cowboy Brock McNeal doesn't date women with kids. So why can't he stop thinking about single-mom Cassie Stanford?*

*Read on for a sneak preview of*
**THE BULL RIDER'S TWIN TROUBLE,**
*the first book in Ali Olson's*
**SPRING VALLEY, TEXAS** *series!*

Brock hurried up the steps to the front porch, noting the squeaking of the stairs and the flaking white paint.

He hoped the widow didn't expect him to be working there too often. If his mother was so desperate to have him around, why would she give him a big job that might eat into all the time he had at home?

Brock brushed the question aside and knocked. He'd go through a short introduction and make his way back for his hot meal, then he'd begin preparing for his next rodeo.

After a few seconds, the door opened and any thought of food or rodeos disappeared. He stared, caught off guard by the lovely woman who stood there.

Her dark brown hair fell around her shoulders in a mass of curls, framing an open, sweet face and lips that promised more than just smiles for the guy lucky enough to get to kiss them.

Brock suddenly felt like an awkward teenager. It took all his effort to arrange his face into a cool, confident

HWREXP1217

smile. "Hello, ma'am," he said, putting on a slightly thicker drawl than usual. "I'm Brock McNeal. My folks live just over the way. They said Mrs. Stanford was in need of some help fixin' up this place, and I thought it best to come introduce myself."

A plan was already formulating in Brock's mind. Make nice to the old lady, get in good with the beautiful mystery woman, then ask her for a date. Easy enough.

The woman smiled. "Nice to meet you. Call me Cassie. Your mother was so sweet to offer your help."

Brock's mind shifted gears quickly. The widow was Cassie.

Before he could say anything, two young boys shot into the doorway, their identical faces peering at him from behind Cassie's legs.

"Zach, Carter, say hello to Mr. McNeal. He'll be helping us fix up the place a bit."

Brock tried his hardest to keep the disappointment off his face, but he wasn't sure he succeeded.

Of course she had kids. There had to be something or his mother would've just come out and told him about her sneaky little plan. She knew well enough by now he didn't plan on having any children, and that meant no dating women with kids, either.

*Don't miss THE BULL RIDER'S TWIN TROUBLE*
*by Ali Olson, available January 2018*
*wherever Harlequin® Western Romance books*
*and ebooks are sold.*

www.Harlequin.com

HWREXP1217